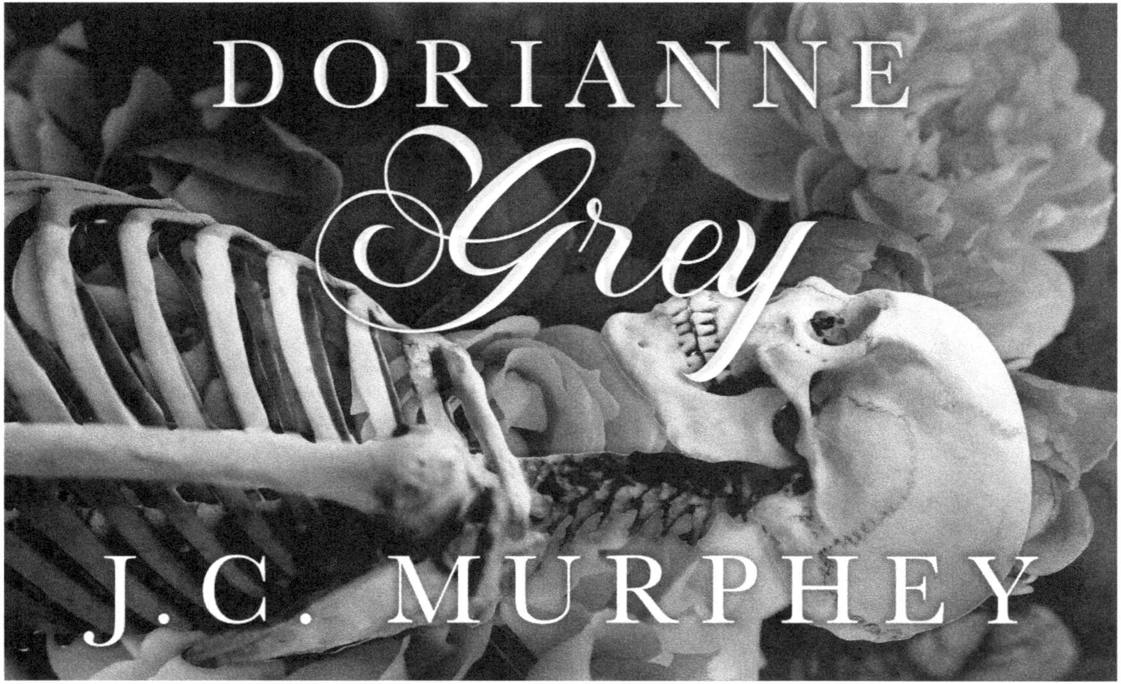

Copyright © 2024 by J.C. Murphey

All rights reserved.

No part of this publication may be reproduced, distributed, or transmitted in any form or by any means, including photocopying, recording, or other electronic or mechanical methods, without the prior written permission of the publisher, except as permitted by U.S. copyright law. For permission requests, contact J.C. Murphey at j.cee.murphey@gmail.com

The story, all names, characters, and incidents portrayed in this production are fictitious. No identification with actual persons (living or deceased), places, buildings, and products is intended or should be inferred.

Book Cover by The Red Fox Creative

Disclaimer

This book contains elements that may not be suitable for all readers. Trigger warnings include explicit sex scenes, gory depictions of murder/crime, profanity, and self-harm.

Below are some free resources for those who need a little extra help. It doesn't make you weak to ask for it. In fact, it makes you brave to share your battle with someone else.

SAMHSA's National Helpline for individuals and families facing mental and/or substance use disorders :
1-800-662-HELP (4357)

988 Lifeline if you're thinking about suicide, are worried about a friend or loved one, or would like emotional support:
Dial or text 988

J.C. MURPHEY

This book is for my loving husband, Sho. Thanks for putting up with my bullshit. And for mopping the floor without me asking. You're the best.

The Sin

Restoration Era, Year 67

"Dorianne, we would love to have you over for this month's full moon ritual. You have been gone for such a long time the other coven members have… been whispering. It's not a good look, sister."

Dylan's face filled the heavy silver hand mirror they communicated through, her expression intent and needlessly impassioned. Surely, she knew that was a low blow. She knew why Dorianne had stepped down as the Black Staff Coven's Crone, not that Dorianne expected her to understand. She saw just as clearly that the newer members—maybe within the last five years—did not join because they shared Dorianne's perspective when it came to the delicate balance of magic and nature.

They joined because they saw her as someone who they could either hide behind to avoid their sordid pasts, or spy on to learn how she gained so much power. Dorianne suspected her own sister was spearheading the latter motivation. In the last few months before she officially stepped down from her position, Dorianne felt there were eyes in every keyhole and ears in every wall.

"I'm sure the members have been whispering," she capitulated. "I hoped that appointing someone as level-headed and decisive as you in my place would have quieted them, though. They seemed to come to you with their thoughts more so than me, when I was still with the coven."

The double-edged answer struck true. Dylan's lips twisted in a sneer for the briefest moment before she schooled her features again. Her little sister had yet to hide her true feelings as well as Dorianne could. Even so, Dorianne was curious about what she was plotting.

"Have you sanctioned this ritual with the officials?"

This time Dylan didn't bother to hide her disgust. "The Supernatural Investigation Agency? Those bumbling fools have no jurisdiction over us. I refuse to acknowledge their self-imposed authority over things they do not know. They can hardly decide how to structure their little group, much less be able to monitor practitioners."

"Whether you acknowledge them or not is irrelevant. If you don't want the coven to be hunted down like a pack of rabid dogs, you will heed their protocols and make sure they are aware of your actions. You are now the Crone of the most powerful collection of witches in the northeast. Use that position to build strong ties with those who do not practice what we do, so they do not lash out in fear."

Her sister's eyes rolled dramatically as she clearly brushed Dorianne's advice away. "I will do what is best for the coven as Crone. It is just as you said, sister, you appointed me yourself."

Dylan hardly considered the SIA a threat to her superior spellcasting abilities. Dorianne didn't want to meddle in the coven's affairs any more than she had to, but she felt compelled to see what it was her sister was getting herself into.

"I'll come."

Dylan's shock was priceless. Her mouth flopped open unattractively, opening and closing a couple times like a fish gasping for air before she could finally respond. "Truly?"

"Yes."

She waited, eyes narrowed, as if expecting Dorianne to add something on. "But? What are your conditions?"

"Nothing," she replied nonchalantly. Dorianne had hardly made direct eye contact throughout the entire conversation, busy making notations in her tome on a recent spell she had been working on for plant growth acceleration using integrated water magic. But she watched in her peripherals when Dylan didn't think she was paying attention, and those were the moments that told her more than anything that came from her sister's mouth. "I am interested to see the direction you have taken the coven since I stepped down."

Dylan beamed, the smile showing a little too much tooth to express happiness. "I'm very sure you will be surprised how far we have come."

The location Dylan had indicated for her to attend the ritual was not particularly suspicious. What was suspicious was that Dylan had refused to give her said location beforehand. She just opened a portal right at Dorianne's front door and expected her to step through it. They may *share blood, but Dorianne didn't trust her enough to blindly walk into a portal with an unknown amount of witches on the other side. Her black tome in hand, Dorianne used a portal reversal she developed herself to find where Dylan intended to take her and casted an untraceable portal of her own within walking distance. She even threw a stuffed bear through as a cheeky response before cutting off Dylan's spell.*

The scene Dorianne now laid eyes on was shocking, to say the least. At least a hundred witches filled the large space, almost a small field more than a natural meadow in the woods. Trunks had been roughly cut down, stumps used to set ritual supplies on, and the flavor of magic that tainted the air tasted foul. When Dorianne had left her leadership in the Black Staff, there was an intimately small number of witches she had allowed to join. Her selection process had been very strict and she rarely let someone in without a reference from a reputable mentor.

This was... unbelievable. There was no way a ritual site of this magnitude would be overlooked by the SIA, much less the skeptical locals. While magic had become more of a common practice in recent years, a clear alienation had grown between the witches who practiced and those who were merely sensitive to it. There was so much the general population didn't know, and society as a whole was just barely pulling itself up by its bootstraps from whatever catastrophic event had brought humanity low.

This was what drove Dorianne to dedicate her life to studying the seemingly-new capability to use magic to bend the natural laws. She wanted to educate people, spreading the fruits of her labor with like-minded practitioners to make everyone's lives easier and more comfortable. That was why she started the Black Staff Coven. Now, she worried Dylan was twisting her dream into a nightmare.

"This is madness, sister," Dorianne murmured to herself and clutched her tome closer.

Just from the brief glance of bleached bone skulls—human skulls—and dark obsidian stone shards that looked sharp enough to cut, along with black and red wax candles and the smoky smell of herbs she couldn't parse, it was obvious the coven planned to cast some horridly dark magic.

The air practically vibrated around her, so potent was her rage. Dorianne could tell where the portal was supposed to deliver her, right in the middle of the group next to a roughly-hewn wooden altar. Dark iron chains were draped across it in preparation to hold something—or someone—down.

"Where is she?" An older witch hissed at Dylan while wrapping a gnarled hand around her bicep. "Is this a fucking joke to you, Dylan?"

The woman didn't even give her the respect of the honorific Crone. Dylan's ire rose, and she barely reigned it in to keep from ripping the impetuous witch's head from her shoulders. Dylan held the brown teddy Dorianne has thrown through the original portal in both hands, so tightly her nails threatened to rip the stuffed animal to shreds, an outright expression of the hatred plain on her face now. Her eyes glowed a dark reddish-black completely unlike the green of her natural-born earth magic. Whatever she was doing, Dylan was already far gone.

Her voice was strained and gravelly. "Damn that pretentious bitch! I should have known she wouldn't just roll over and die. Has anyone managed to track her down?" Dylan called out to the crowd around her. "Don't just stand around waiting for handouts, you fucking vultures! Go find her!"

The vitriol spewing from her was poisonous, tainting any memory of her sister that seemed innocent and pure. Dorianne hardly recognized the younger woman barking orders and insults in equal parts as she threw the bear to the ground. It immediately burst into black and purple flames and fell to ashes in a breath. She knew Dylan was ambitious and jealous. She knew her sister was responsible for the beginning of this power-hungry shift in the coven's mentality. But she didn't realize how far Dylan was willing to go to gain that power she felt was robbed from her at birth. She could never accept that Dorianne was stronger because she pushed herself to such incredible lengths to grow and understand magic. All she saw was her older sister have accolades rained down upon her for something Dylan herself felt she couldn't obtain.

It was not safe here. Dorianne needed to get back to the safety of her well-warded house. In a knee-jerk reaction, she spun from the tree she had been hiding behind and threw her hand open for a portal to whisk her away to safety.

A portal she didn't bother to hide.

Dylan's keen senses picked up on the unique flavor of Dorianne's magic as soon as the first wisp of it was released. She honed in on the shadowy perimeter and found Dorianne about to slip from her grasp yet again.

"Not this time, sister!" She shot across the clearing in a bolt of black lightning, hitting Dorianne square between the shoulder blades with enough brutality to throw them both into a thick tree trunk. Dylan's hands snatched both her wrists in an icy grip and wrenched her arms back with inhuman strength. Dorianne howled in agony as both the shoulders popped from their sockets with sickening crunches and the tendons stretched almost to snapping. "You're not escaping your fate, Dorianne," she snarled. "Your power will be MINE!"

The pain had stunned Dorianne long enough—only a few heartbeats, really—for the rest of the hungry pack to fall upon her, dragging her limp body from Dylan's clutches and casting their own spells to further neutralize her, fuzzing her mind and taking her vision with more burning. Her back slammed down onto a rough, hard surface. Every feeble thrash she attempted only resulted in splinters piercing through her clothes until even those were ripped off. The witches looped chains around any limb they could touch and locked them down.

Then, they descended upon her with their tools. The ones she had warily taken notice of on the cut stumps.

The wolfish coven started with her face. Specifically, her mouth. She tried to snap her teeth around fingers that had reached to pinch her mouth shut but was too weak to do much more than barely open her lips. A wide bone needle threaded with rough black thread pierced through the top right corner of Dorianne's lip and out the bottom one. That piercing burst of pain was enough to jolt her brain from its magic-induced fog enough to scream, eyes stretched open wide but refusing to leak tears.

If only she knew that was the last time she would see the night sky in this lifetime.

The more malicious members took those obsidian daggers to her eyes, hacking at them until they were nothing but oozing sacs they had dug from the sockets and eaten whole. Then they went after the fingers, then the organs they ripped from her lower torso. Everything but her heart.

Eventually the pain overloaded Dorianne's mind. That's all there was. It was a small mercy she went into shock, systems shutting down in an effort to preserve whatever sanity she would be able to keep at the bitter end.

She hoped they choked on her. Just like they choked on her ideals of being satisfied with the magic they had, instead of greedy for what a witch should never touch.

"Rot in hell, sister." Dylan's voice was animalistic in her ear. No longer was she even a human, much less a little sister. Dorianne grit her teeth behind lips sewn shut.

You will join me there, Dylan.

The final desecration, the last crime to pure earth magic they had both made a pact to maintain, was a brutal strike to Dorianne's heart. A *jagged and cold weapon stabbed through her breastbone to add the last element to this unholy ritual.*

Death. At last.

Fluttering her eyelids open again was a jolting experience, to say the least. The last time Dorianne checked, the dead didn't open their eyes. The next shock was what she was looking up at, a sky so clear and blue and bright she had a sneaking suspicion it was fake. She parted her lips cautiously, her jaw unclenching, and stretched the locked muscles in the hollows beneath her cheekbones. With a groan, Dorianne propped herself up on her elbows to assess the rest of the damage she had felt but couldn't see.

There was nothing. She was dressed in a simple black sheath that pooled around her with its baggy size and nothing else. No blood. No cuts. And all of her fingers were accounted for. If anything, they looked much less wrinkled and spotted with age than they had when she lost them, as a witch advancing into her later sixties who spent a lot of time gardening in the sun without gloves. Then she looked around, head swiveling on a limber neck to take in her surroundings, of which there was not much to note. Blue extended as far as the eye could see, as if the sky met the ground in all directions with nothing to break the horizon.

Ahead of her was the only other object of interest to break the skyline. What appeared to be some kind of structure that once sat on two massive red pillars but had fallen in on itself, two black beams stretched between them at a broken angle. Maybe they had once been a door, or perhaps a gate of some sort. It must have been magnificent to look at once upon a time, judging from how tall it was as crumbled pieces of its former glory.

"Welcome, Crone Dorianne Grey."

The voice, as gentle and soothing as it sounded, still made her almost jump from her skin in surprise. Just a second ago she didn't think anyone was in this strange, peaceful place. But as she turned her head to find the owner of the voice, Dorianne was greeted with far more than she could have possibly expected.

Two figures stood there, one towering much higher than the one who was closer to Dorianne. Both were shrouded in robes so dark they appeared shadow-like, but the shorter person was dressed much more elaborately. The cloak—or maybe a robe, given the sleeves covering their arms—had a seamless gradient from black to a blood red at the bottom, parted to reveal sandaled feet and loose black pants that cinched at the ankles. Dorianne's eyes drifted back up the stranger's body, catching again on their torso.

Her *torso*.

Red ropes—at least as thick as a wrist twisted together with some kind of silky-looking thread—crossed over her chest between a modest bust and wrapped around, over and over until they overlapped two or three times. A simple black top could barely be seen underneath beyond the thin piece of fabric stretching up to cover half her throat. They looked... heavy. Dorianne imagined hunching under the weight of all that rope, but the woman stood straight and with a confident air. From her back, what appeared to be thousands of those individual red strands that made up the rope flared behind her like wings, wafting gently in a breeze that wasn't there and extending up until they faded to nothing. They seemed to glow with some kind of golden sheen and were mesmerizing to watch.

It wasn't the ropes that were oppressive, though. It was the miasma looming behind her like a giant beast hovering over its prey, writhing *and lashing out with whip-like tendrils and the hint of clawed hands reaching toward her. The sheer amount of magical aura oozing from it was enough to make even Dorianne, a powerful witch in her own right, feel ill at ease. Actually, this flavor of magic was not wholly unlike that which Dylan seemed to be dabbling in.*

Dylan...

"I'm not a Crone anymore," Dorianne finally answered, still sitting in her prone position turned toward the pair. "I'm not much of anything anymore, am I? Is this the afterlife?"

The second person snorted, a distinctly low-pitched sound like that of a man. "That's everyone's question, huh?"

She couldn't see it, but Dorianne had the impression the woman rolled her eyes beneath the lip of a hood hiding her face in shadow.

"Ignore him. He's my personal retribution for bad choices."

"She's just bitter because I occasionally make her laugh," the man retorted in his rumbling voice. Compared to the woman, he seemed very rigid in his stance, bracing his thick legs shoulder-width apart and crossing his arms across a broad chest. Muscles bulged beneath the smooth, dark skin peeking out from beneath the loose sleeves of his own robe. He obviously took a guardian role to this woman, despite the heckling.

Dorianne was tired of holding her head tilted at this awkward angle. Whatever bullshit she felt she was fixing to deal with, she wanted to do it standing on her own feet. But when she went to lift her arms and pull up, her arms were met with an immovable weight. Or more specifically, she was being held down with an immovable weight. Dorianne tried her feet next.

Nothing.

She was totally stuck.

Panicked, her head whipped down to find what was restraining her, half afraid to see the chains that had bound her to the altar remained in death. Dylan would be that petty, if it were possible to torture Dorianne further by doing so. No, what held her down was what she had originally assumed to be a smooth floor. Seeing how it rippled slightly with every frantic jerk of her arms, Dorianne realized it was more than just that.

It looked like... water. But also more than water. She looked beyond the surface where her forearms had already sunk past to the tops of the elbows, and the sight made her go cold to the bone.

People were floating beneath the glass-like surface. Ghostly and semi-transparent, their eyes were closed as if sleeping and hands crossed across their chest. There had to be thousands, if not millions of them, going so far and so deep her brain could hardly comprehend the number.

Now was finally the time to panic! Yes, panic now! *Dorianne's brain screamed at her*, knocking her loose from the dazed stare the souls had sucked her into.

"Get me out of here! Out, OUT! *Drasili mok guel ta wurin*—" Dorianne uttered a spell she hoped would release her from whatever paralyzed her body.

"Magic will not release you, witch." The woman kept her voice calm. "Only I can."

Now Dorianne showed her rage. "Then get me out, you damn demon! Or I swear—"

The man laughed again. "Please, do finish that threat. I'd love a good catfight."

"What the hell is a catfight? Ugh!" She shook her head in frustration and continued to thrash about as much as she could to get loose. "Never mind, just tell me what you did to me!"

"I didn't do anything." The man held his hands up by his head, palms facing Dorianne in a placating manner. "That's all her."

"Yes, and I need your assistance," the woman elaborated.

Dorianne's head snapped around and she glowered at the hooded stranger. "What? I'm dead, aren't I? Not much I can do from here, is there?"

"Not if you agree to help me."

She wished the woman would at least pull her hood down, to gauge the seriousness of her face personally. "Again, with what?"

The dark shadows behind her flailed even more now, as if they had caught the scent of fresh blood and became excited from it. Now the strain was obvious in the slight stiffening of the small woman's shoulders. Maybe she was holding it back?

"I need... a vessel," she began, almost hesitantly. "A vicious horde of demons was set upon the mortal world that took a great sacrifice to capture, and I have held them back as long as I can in my current state. I cannot recover to my full strength as their host, but I cannot let them run rampant or banish them to hell to be utilized yet again. So... I come to you, Crone, with an offer. Unspeakable power and control over their shadow and death magic capabilities, in return for serving as their living host. A pact-bearer, as you humans call it, with this demon horde."

Said horde responded with multiple heads forming from the mass hovering behind her, maws ripping open in silent howls of rage. Their agitated roiling made the woman fall forward slightly, just a small step forward with shoulders now hunched. Her companion laid a hand on her shoulder that she immediately grasped with one of her own. The more the shadows grew and fought, the more of a toll it seemed to take on her. It seemed like too much of a burden for Dorianne to bear.

"For how long?"

The woman chuckled stiffly at that. "Very shrewd. Unfortunately, I do not have an answer. At least, not a pleasant one. It will probably be for the rest of time, or however long your soul can hold them. But something tells me we have a similar... indomitable will, so to speak. The more spellcasting you utilize the demons' power with, the easier they will be to manage."

"If it was that easy, why don't you do it?"

"I don't need spells to accomplish my purpose. Therefore, they are... building up, accumulating more power as they try to drain me of mine."

The demonic heads behind her thrashed again, excitedly.

"And if I don't agree to this?"

"You don't wanna know," the man answered drolly. Then he pointed down at the lifeless, floating bodies. That was enough for Dorianne.

"Not much of a choice," she muttered. Her head fell back and she sighed heavily, looking up at the perfectly blue sky again. "I suppose I will make this deal with the devil."

The man put in his opinion yet again. She failed to see how he was so chipper about this subject. "Oh-ho-ho, she probably drives a harder bargain than him."

Dorianne's head lifted, and the woman was right in front of her now, looming over her prone body. Even at this angle she couldn't see the face inside the hood. That was, until the woman lowered it to reveal something beside a face entirely.

It was unlike anything Dorianne had ever seen, even as one who studied nature and everything that resided in it. A skull covered her face, in life some kind of large bird with jagged teeth along the edges of its beak that had to be longer than her hand from the tip of her longest finger to wrist. Across the bleached white surface were the etchings of a script, both spiked and curling as it ran vertically in neat rows. The most unsettling of the whole sight was what laid within the eye sockets. Eyes lit from deep within the skull, flickering along the edges as if they were made of pale blue flames themselves.

Slowly, she reached a hand down to rest lightly on Dorianne's forehead, the sleeve of the cloak falling away to reveal skin so white it looked skeletal.

"Through the will of Azrael, you now carry this burden." She paused, voice even but solemn. "Thank you, Crone Grey."

The heaving shadows flowed down the outstretched arm, a massive flea hopping from one host to another. Her last horrifying sight before blacking out was the gaping maw of a beast whose teeth ringed all the way down to a void inside its throat, rushing down the woman's arm to swallow Dorianne whole. It's mouth engulfed her in a pain that was incomprehensible, even compared to what she had experienced in her last memorable moments of life as a ritual sacrifice. The monster ate more than her body. It devoured her very soul and merged itself with it, recreating her entire existence.

They were sucked through the dead waters all together, falling farther and farther from the light the woman Azrael *stood in, her hand still outstretched as if she were the one propelling them through the floating souls to punch out the other side.*

Back to the world of the living, but no longer alive among them.

Chapter One

Restoration Era, Year 202

"Day-um. This is raunchy. Leave it to batshit crazy witches to find creative ways to kill someone."

Trackers Robert Jennison and Jamie Lewis, bundled in their dark gray agency-standard jackets, picked their way along the border of the crime scene with neon yellow tape that glowed subtly in the dark night, the thinnest sliver of moon offering little light. As they met on the other side of the starting point, the connected ends snapped together with a *hiss* and flared brighter, creating an enchanted barrier to preserve the scene from trespassers and nosy reporters. The shimmering dome served as a warning, visible to even the least magic-sensitive humans, to avoid running into it and suffering some excruciating repercussions.

"No kidding," his partner muttered, brushing her hands down the sides of her jacket as if to wipe off dirt. Just standing next to the site made her feel unclean. "Every time I get called out for an unsanctioned ritual site I get the creeps. Some things you just don't mess with, you know?"

The man scoffed and scrubbed at the dark beginnings of a beard on his cheek. "Wouldn't be sanctioned if it didn't fuck with the laws of nature. Any more than practitioners already do, anyway. C'mon, Lewis, let's sit in the car until the uppers get here. Imma lose a finger soon in this goddamn cold."

"Why don't you use your pockets, Jennison?"

Amidst their good-natured squabbling, another car pulled up, windows tinted so dark the driver was hidden. As it glided to a silent stop, a cloud of red-tinted steam hissed behind from the exhaust pipes. Nothing in particular marked the sleek black sedan, but the two officers straightened to attention as the driver and passenger doors swung open.

"Agent Yarrow, good evening," Agent Lewis called out and checked her blonde hair was slicked back into its high ponytail before stepping forward to shake the hands of their visitors. "Just secured the crime scene. Doesn't look like anyone stumbled on it before we got here. The residual magic lit up the tracking spell like it was on fire. Nasty spellcasting, whoever did this."

"Thank you," the older woman nodded to the two officers and turned to her own partner. The no-nonsense cut of her gray bob framed her face, creases at the corners of her mouth and eyes telling of a light humor and easy smile. "This is Investigator Theo Slater. He's been training with me for the last three months as handler for our profiling consultant, so go easy on the newbie," she teased lightly and shoved her hands into the pockets of her heavy jacket. "I filled him in on the info he needs to collect, so Theo will be taking over from here."

Her friendly face was a direct counterweight to her more serious—and much younger—partner. Arms crossed over his chest was the universal sign for "I don't want to chat," and coupled with a stern expression made for a particularly unwelcome introduction. Unruly dark brown hair fell across his forehead and hid the tops of his ears, but nothing could detract from the piercing hawk-like gaze of light hazel eyes beneath his brow furrowed in a natural glower.

Jennison cleared his throat. "Right. Er, based on our initial evaluation it appears this ritual took place two nights ago, on the last new moon. Hope you haven't eaten yet. It's pretty graphic."

"If it caused such a dramatic reaction from the tracking spell, that would be expected," came the smooth response from over Yarrow's shoulder.

Theo's attention moved to the ritual site as he replied, taking in all the gore and blood spattered among the tree stumps and wilted grass in the clearing. Eyes sharpened, the golden-hazel of them darkened even further with concentration as if committing every gruesome detail to memory.

Agent Lewis stepped aside, giving him a clearer view of the scene. "That's our assumption as well. Don't get a lot of ritualistic sacrifices these days."

"You do, but they're better at hiding than this group," Theo said. Lewis bristled at the cool response. Theo had already brushed past her to stand at the edge of the barrier tape. "Almost as if... they want to be found," he mused to himself.

As far as crime scenes went, this was the most gory Theo had been called out for to date. The roster wasn't extensive, but his introduction to the world of ritual investigation in the last three months was tame in comparison to this one. Almost theatrically set, from his experience. A burly man—maybe thirty, the same age as Theo—lay tied down by coarse black rope to a massive wooden altar propped up by several stumps, recently cut down judging by the shavings of wood scattered on the hard-packed dirt. The large radius of crushed grass indicated there could have been a large crowd of people involved to carry it out, but no tracks—human or vehicle—seemed to have disturbed the brittle grass around the clearing except for those belonging to the cars here now.

Everything seemed to have been made from trees cut down in this very clearing, from the bloody altar itself to the stumps that made for makeshift tables littered with goblets and all manners of sharp tools. Who had the time—or manpower—to accomplish all this in a single night? Surely, this many people gathered together would have drawn attention from the locals if there had been a constant coming and going for preparations.

"Any reports of missing persons? Perhaps within a hundred miles? Most portals can't reach beyond that." His question once again caught the first responders off-guard. They hurried to their car to report in with a scrying mirror for an answer from the research team.

Agent Yarrow stood aside, arms crossed, with a pleased smirk on her face. Theo had taken to this line of work as quickly as she thought he would. When she had announced her retirement to Captain Tate, she had feared finding a replacement would be next to impossible. The consultant they used required very... specific information to be able to profile possible suspects. Beyond the above-average skills of deduction, the agent needed to have a solid foundation of tracking magic users.

That was the sole purpose of the Supernatural Investigation Agency, to track down practitioners who toed the line of what nature allowed them to manipulate using magic. And of the thirty-two years Rebecca Yarrow dedicated to the SIA, she had yet to find a more talented and naturally-gifted tracker as Theo Slater. His distinct lack of spellcasting experience—a damn shame in her opinion considering his potential—did not detract from his ability to take over this job.

She wished she knew what kept him from developing his magic, but he was as impenetrable as the strongest fortress. Rebecca only worried that his cleverness and propensity for being extremely curious would get him into trouble with the elusive witch they employed for profiling.

Lost in her thoughts, Rebecca failed to notice Theo had already stepped onto the scene, pen and a small leather-bound notebook in his hands as he picked through the clearing. Agent Lewis looked to be having a minor stroke.

"How... he..." she sputtered. "How did he get through that barrier! That's a Level 5 ward! It's supposed to keep out organic and inorganic matter of any size!"

"Yes, yes," Rebecca responded, rolling her hand casually. "He has a tendency to toe the line when it comes to rules and such. Just leave him be. Theo knows to keep the evidence intact for the research unit. Speaking of, how far off are they?"

Even as she reassured the agent, Theo kicked a rock over to peer beneath, causing Lewis to pale an even lighter shade in horror. Rebecca struggled to keep in the chuckle trying to escape her pursed lips. His lack of regard was entertaining, to say the least. She trusted Theo to keep the integrity of the site that mattered.

"How goes it, Theo?" she called out in some semblance of monitoring—mostly for Lewis's sake. Rebecca knew he had it under control.

He had been leaning over the unfortunate sacrifice, documenting the limbs that had been brutally sawed off and placed at strategic locations in the remnants of the magic array etched on the ground around him. Judging from the pained terror frozen on the victim's face, the parts had been removed while he was still alive. Gruesome, indeed. She very rarely saw witches who went after the genitalia quite as brutally as the ones who performed this ritual. Rebecca watched on with a motherly sense of pride as Theo picked his way around the ritual site, noting the various runes etched into strategically-placed tree stumps and their relation to the scattered body parts.

"I have what I need," Theo responded tersely a few minutes later, stepping straight through the barrier again as if it didn't exist. She had her suspicions about where his little barrier-nullifying quirk came from, but the captain refused to answer any questions even as he dropped the fledgling agent into her lap as her replacement.

Jennison shook his head at the audacity. "Kids these days. Can't even follow the basic laws of magic anymore."

"Come along now, Theo!" Rebecca chirped brightly and tipped her head to the stunned duo. "Don't want to keep the ol' girl waiting now, do we? She has a thing for being punctual."

"Right," Theo replied. "Nice to meet you, Agents Jennison and Lewis. I look forward to working with you in the future."

Just as suddenly as they burst into the clearing, the two agents swept back into their car and bumped down the dirt road back through the forest. A cloud of steam trailed behind as a testament to how much exertion the rough terrain forced out of the magically-powered vehicle.

"Theo Slater, huh?" Jennison's gruff voice rumbled in the cool air. His forearms leaned against the roof as he stared at the car leaving the scene, the reckless driving indicating Rebecca at the wheel. "'Like father, like son' is right."

"Did you say something?"

Lewis was busy in the car, scribbling notes furiously on her pad to reword later in their scene report. She certainly couldn't expect Jennison to file it in a timely manner, and she was tired of getting in trouble for his lackadaisical habits. Within the two minutes since their guests departed, it looked like her head had been caught in a twister, pieces of blonde strands flying every which direction.

She must be stressed.

"Nuthin', Lewis. Move over. I'll drive so you can work on the report to the captain."

"How kind of you."

Jennison bit back his smile at her snide reply and climbed into the driver's side, placing his hand on the dash to ignite the steam-magic engine.

"Never thought I'd see the day Rebecca Yarrow left the force."

Lewis shrugged, eyes set to her page as Jennison turned the car around to face the narrow road. "The SIA has changed since she came in. Maybe she can't hang with it anymore. I know I find myself reconsidering my life choices in this field sometimes."

"A lot has changed," he agreed absently. "My own parents didn't even have cars growing up. Magic has definitely helped humanity get back on its feet since... well, since the Extermination."

Everyone learned the basics in school about the Extermination Event. Agents in the Supernatural Investigation Agency got a more in-depth course, since a lot of what they dealt with was a direct consequence of it. Over two hundred years ago, every living thing on Earth was wiped out as far as anyone could tell. Killed. Eliminated. Whatever word the big brains at the universities like to use to describe the phenomenon of every living animal suddenly dying en masse. Some speculated toxic gas being released into the atmosphere. Others thought it was some kind of electromagnetic pulse used as a weapon of mass destruction.

No one, however, knew exactly what happened. Every day old documents were being unearthed, restored and studied in an effort to find the history that was lost before two-hundred-odd years ago. As far as SIA could tell, it seemed like one day people and animals just reappeared again, as if they had taken a vacation for some unknown time then come back. Humanity just picked itself where they left off, and at an accelerated speed rebuilt the machinery that had been left behind by the previous civilization. From studying and taking apart the old cars and equipment found in massive factories and stranded on roads, humans were able to reverse-engineer the technology that had been lost with a twist.

Now, humans had magic.

It didn't seem like magic was practiced—or even available—before the Extermination. How they lived like that was beyond Jennison's comprehension. Where did energy to power houses come from? How did people protect themselves without wards? How did agents even find crime scenes without tracker spells? Just the day-to-day living sounded impossible without magic to help.

The only physical alteration humans seemed to have after the Extermination to denote a capacity for magic were black cracks appearing in the irises of newborn practitioners, otherwise known as shatter-patterns. The thicker the jagged lines a person's shatter-pattern was, the stronger their abilities to control magic seemed to be. Trackers like Jennison, Lewis, and the new guy Theo had almost non-existent patterns in their eyes, denoting their weaker spellcasting but higher sensitivity to magic use. Most of the SIA agents with stronger patterns tended to land in the research or tactical units that utilized their stronger casting abilities for offensive or healing spells.

Of course, with that kind of power came people who couldn't be responsible or humble enough to stay in their lane and not try to fuck it up for everyone else. Or in the case of the ritual victim, not drag some innocent person into their bullshit for more power.

"... attach a copy of the drawing from the consultant?"

"Eh?" Jennison wasn't paying attention to whatever Lewis had asked him.

She sighed, fed up with Jennison's lack of attention. "I said, 'Can you attach a copy of the drawing from the consultant when the new guy sends it over?' so I can put your name on this report as having done something?"

"Yeah yeah, ya damn harpy. I'll get the files put together. Don't worry your pretty head over it."

He hoped they could track down whoever planned that fucked-up ritual. It was more than just the deplorable state the poor victim was left in. Something about the residual energies in that clearing gave him a horrible feeling in his chest and a foul taste in his mouth, feeling tainted just breathing the air touched by that dark magic.

These witches were bad news. Jennison didn't need a tracker spell to tell him that.

"Here we are."

Rebecca smoothly parked the car in front of a plain-looking brownstone in a plain-looking Salem suburb rebuilt in the last twenty years. Not really what Theo was expecting for some all-powerful witch who liked to live in complete seclusion. How did she avoid anyone right in the middle of a neighborhood? Surely, the SIA wouldn't let a supposedly-dangerous witch just sit pretty among these unassuming people.

"No creepy forest trail leading up to an old hut? I'm disappointed." He peered out the windows on either side of the car, taking in the elderly couple strolling along the sidewalk across the street and some children playing in a park near the corner. It all felt very... pedestrian. Almost too much so.

Even saying that, he could sense some kind of looming presence—something unnatural and dangerous that yelled at anyone who approached to get lost—emanating from the home. Like being watched by a predator in the dark but not knowing exactly where the threat of an attack was. While Theo didn't portray any outward magical abilities, he had an acute awareness of magic that lingered after spellcasting that helped him when investigating crime scenes. Since he could sense it this far away, he knew there was a monumental amount of magic being used for something.

"Sometimes things best hidden are those that blend in," Rebecca responded vaguely. "Now, let's drop off your notes so we can go get my retirement milkshake from that diner downtown!" Her demeanor was entirely too chipper for just visiting that gruesome ritual site. Maybe it was a defense mechanism, a way she coped with what had to have been decades of dealing with the twisted minds of dark witches for as long as she had. The SIA only called Rebecca in for the most complex unsanctioned rituals, from what Theo understood in his on-boarding.

"I wasn't aware we were getting milkshakes."

"Well, now you are. And you're treating."

Theo followed after her and climbed the three steps to a dark wooden door. From afar it looked like some ornate etchings made a flowing, curling pattern along the surface. As Theo moved closer, the patterns became more apparent that they were more than just fancy script. Every one was a hieroglyphic rune commonly used by practitioners—casually known as witches. Nothing too out of place for someone who practiced magic. However, one spiked symbol near the doorbell looked particularly ominous.

"Is this witch a light or dark practitioner?"

Theo's question, however abrupt it seemed, did not surprise Rebecca. Out of all the applicants clambering to be selected as her successor, she chose him for this sharp sense of observation—beyond the fact he was obviously a good choice at Captain Tate's recommendation. She hoped that skill wouldn't land him in hot water with their resident witch. She was a prickly one.

"I'd say this one is somewhere in the gray," she answered, lips curled into a wry smile at her little joke. "She's powerful because she doesn't let herself be defined by the kind of magic she wields. From our understanding—and by our, I mainly mean the research group at SIA—she seems proficient with all known elements of magic use. But among the pact-bearers, she is known as the Mother of Shadows."

"That doesn't sound at all menacing." Theo's response was equal parts droll and wary. "And we don't really know *why* she's called that, do we?"

"Right-o." Rebecca clapped him on the back with her right hand while reaching out to the doorbell button with the other. "Hence the reason my job, soon to be your job, exists. While I hesitate to call ourselves spies on her doorstep, we essentially keep tabs on her while also acting as the go-between to get some info on potential suspects since she doesn't go to scenes herself. No one has met her face to face, as far as I'm aware. Even after my twenty-four years as her handler, *I* haven't seen Dorianne's face. I just come to her door and hand over my notes, then pick up the drawings she slips out the mail slot to find our suspects. They haven't been wrong yet."

Theo nodded, seemingly satisfied with her answer. Or at least mollified. "That's her name, Dorianne?"

"Yep, Dorianne Grey." They were almost done with the exchange, and Rebecca was seriously craving that milkshake. "Okay, rip your page out and press it face-down to the door, where that smooth part is." She gestured to the small rectangle about chest-level with Theo, lined with scrawling black runes. They almost blended in with the dark grain of the door.

He glanced at the space skeptically but followed her directions. "Okay..."

She snickered at his yelp of shock as the door flashed a shocking yellow, sucking the page through with an efficient *snap* of the paper. The wood rippled, like a puddle's surface lightly disturbed, before solidifying to its regular texture.

"Honestly, Theo, of all the things you've seen, a spell like this on a door surprises you?"

"Excuse the hell out of me, *Rebecca*. I haven't been in the field as long as you. I didn't deal with much beyond practical household magic before getting this job."

Rebecca ruffled his hair affectionately. "Yeah yeah, ya' whippersnapper. Come on, our work is done for now. We'll be back for the sketch tomorrow."

"That's it?"

"Why? You wanna try knocking on the door?"

He gave the carved-up wood another wary glance. "No thanks. I can't even tell what any of these runes say. I'd rather not die today if I can help it."

"Good call."

The watchful eye of a woman just on the other side of the protective door peered curiously through the invisible peephole as they climbed back into their car and drove away. Bending from her towering height, she plucked the page retrieved from her spell and held it up between her pointer finger and thumb to read.

"Theo Slater..." Her voice was quiet and low, just above a whisper in the mausoleum-like home. She studied the no-nonsense slant of his penmanship, every letter sharp and curves tight and controlled. Even his signature at the bottom seemed proper and impersonal. He already piqued her interest. "I look forward to working with you."

Chapter Two

"Terror has struck Salem again with the discovery of missing person Richard Collins, 32, in a nearby forest Friday evening. According to the SIA, he was brutally murdered and his body used in an unsanctioned ritual on the night of the full moon. They believe this is one in a series of failed rituals by a coven of dark magic practitioners. Details have yet to be discovered." A well-dressed pair of news anchors turned from the board behind them showing some of the more tame pictures from the crime scene to face the viewers. They had been going on and on about this juicy piece for hours, ever since Theo walked through the door to his modest flat early that evening.

A whirring, mechanical sound clicked from the kitchen pantry right on its scheduled time at eight-thirty. The door slid open inside its wall pocket to allow Theo's MAED, a Mechanized and Automated Enchanted Drone, to roll out on metal rollers and inch over to the fridge to await further instructions. Most everything in the modern house was touch or thought-activated, including the MAED. Even someone as magically stunted as Theo could utilize household magic. He sent his dinner out with a silent thought, to which the MAED responded promptly in beginning the preparations of a simple dinner—dry leafy salad and grilled chicken. "While details remain unclear, officials recommend using caution when traveling at night, especially alone. The Collins family offered no comment to the news of their oldest son, but are well-known earth pact-bearers in the—"

Theo sighed heavily and waved his hand toward the television set to shut it off, the power coils spiraling on either side of the screen dimming from their bright red glow as it responded. Every channel spewed the same rhetoric about some dark coven on the loose, surely trying to whip everyone into a fear-induced frenzy. Theo knew for a fact the Captain hadn't released anything about suspects, as Theo hadn't heard from the consultant to go pick up her drawing yet. The news channels were grasping at straws speculating about these cases. In some instances, they made shit up altogether.

"Damn vultures," he grumbled and slouched into the overstuffed armchair from the family home with a piping hot mug of chamomile tea. Apparently it had been his grandmother's, and even with the gaudy blue floral pattern and threadbare spots covered with patches, Theo couldn't bear to part with it. The house was sold long ago and profits put into the trust he now lived off of, so any little piece of his childhood he held onto ferociously.

Just as he lifted the mug to take a hearty sip, his scrying compact gave a mighty vibration from the coffee table on which it sat, the metal of its cover clattering loudly on the polished wood. There were very few people who had a direct link to his personal scrying mirror, and most of them were either asleep or dealing with their own families.

It was the witch. Dorianne Grey.

"Of course it's this late at night when she calls." Theo reached for the compact—just small enough to fit in the palm of his hand—and flipped it open. Instead of a face as he expected, only words floated into view on the small mirror's surface. His lips moved as he read the message silently.

I'm ready.

Of course, she would keep it vague. Surely, she could come up with some other message that couldn't be taken so poorly out of context. 'I'm ready' sounded like they were meeting for some sordid affair. Rebecca didn't give much in the way of what this consultant was like beyond being extremely private, but something about this simple message felt very cheeky. Like she was playing with him. Even so, those two enticing words stirred a curious beast that slumbered until his first visit to her house. When he sensed that intoxicating, heady power exuding from it, he immediately wanted more. Magic like that was addictive.

He anticipated a few rounds of pointed exchanges of wit before she treated him like a partner. Whatever may come with that title. Absently, his fingers played with a loose thread on the armrest of his inherited chair as he stared at the mirror. Unbidden, memories of playing with those loose threads while listening to a nighttime story from his mom intercepted his wandering thoughts. He didn't keep the chair for fuzzy sentimental purposes.

He kept it to remind him of his parents' lives cut too short. Of a childhood robbed from him at seven, when he barely collected enough warm memories to hold onto. This chair was one of the only pieces in their old living room that wasn't drenched in blood at the scene of the murder of Lara and Thomas Slater, two in a long string of cold cases left in a dusty police archive. Their unsolved deaths became his whole purpose, his goal for every step of his life, and the reason he took a two-year criminal justice program at the community college and went straight to the police academy to claw his way up the ranks to detective. He knew it would be hard. The Revived Colonies didn't allow officers under the age of twenty-one to even enter the academy if they exhibited as low of a magic ability as he did, and waiting until his birthday to enroll was excruciating to say the least.

Waiting was the hardest part. Everything else—the physical ability test, the written exams, promotion through the ranks to detective—was easier than he expected. He always knew where to place his foot next to get one step closer to dusting off his parents' murders.

In just six years, Theo's success rate was so astronomically high for the Salem Police Department it caught the eye of a recruiter for the Supernatural Investigation Agency. Now here he sat, working with a consultant he had heard whispers of among the trackers, who could find any criminal the agency set her on.

This was it. If she couldn't help him find who killed his parents, Theo decided more drastic measures needed to be taken. Maybe measures outside what the agency deemed acceptable, even.

The compact buzzed in his hand again, insistent enough to knock Theo from his dazed stare at the coffee table.

"Alright, alright, I'm coming," he muttered, shoving up off the chair to change into something beside pajama pants and a t-shirt.

Theo's sleek black car slid up silently to the curb in front of the witch's brownstone only hours after his first visit—twenty minutes after her ambiguous message thanks to the empty streets—and spewed its red steam as he shifted it into park. This late at night, the neighborhood took on a much darker mood than the friendly façade from earlier. "I'm going to be annoyed if I have to file a report tonight," Theo muttered as he cut off the engine with a wave of his hand across the dash.

He popped his collar against the night's chill when he stepped from the warm interior, walking around the front to the cracked sidewalk. Theo shoved his hands into his coat pockets and stalked up the short set of stairs to the front door.

Just as he raised his hand to press the doorbell, the edge of an envelope poked out from the mail slot halfway down the door. It was like the witch had been waiting to deliver it to him. Despite every other house on the block seeming to run off magic-powered bulb lights on their porches, this was the only one with a purple flame flickering in its glass prison. The dancing light casted eerie shadows against the deep carvings scrawled over the dark wooden door.

"Keeping odd hours, are we?" Theo asked gruffly, not moving to take the paper yet.

There was a short beat of silence, then the muffled response of what seemed like a chuckle permeated through the wood. "I do my best work at night."

Even distorted as it was, the casual tone and low pitch of her voice shocked Theo. He hadn't really expected a response, so to hear her voice at all was a treat. He assumed someone like her had a lilting, dainty sound, belonging to a frail woman too sickly to leave her home. The sound of it was soothing, satisfying in a way Theo couldn't quite put his finger on. It struck just the right chords in his brain to reverberate pleasantly through his body.

"That so?" His reply was light despite the burning curiosity to see the owner of the smooth voice. "Am I going to need to shift my work schedule in kind?"

"I didn't say you needed to pick up the packet tonight. I just said I was ready."

"Fair point." The paper shifted slightly in the slot, so she was still holding on to it. Theo decided to try his luck. "Are you not going to invite me in?"

Her response was immediate, but still light-hearted. "Not unless you want to be material for my next ritual."

Interesting. And very insincere. "Is that a threat?"

"It depends on your intentions, I suppose. Are you sticking your nose where it doesn't belong, or do you mean to cause me harm?"

"Maybe I just want to know who I'm working with."

"Hmmm..."

"Do you at least have a name?"

Theo didn't know why he was pushing so hard for information. Rebecca had already told him, but it felt important for her to tell him herself. To speak for herself. She probably didn't get to do it often. Even in the first three months Theo worked at SIA, rumors were recirculated to reach his ears about the elusive, mysterious consultant who dabbled in dark magic. But something about this first conversation felt important, like it would set the whole tone of their working relationship if he let her hide in her dodgy answers.

He didn't want to just talk to a door for the rest of his assignment. Theo was hungry for more.

The envelope pushed farther out the mail slot, far enough to be held by the flap without assistance. Suddenly, the heaviness in the air ebbed away, like the tide moving out from a shore. The faint rustle of heavy fabric and muffled footfalls on carpet told him the mysterious witch moved away from the door and retreated into the depths of her home.

Was she *the source of that stifling power? Or was it just for show?*

The thought lingered as he pulled the envelope free of its trap, gave the house one last appraising look, and turned hesitantly to walk back to the waiting car.

The thick paper in his hand had that familiar charged tingle, the telltale sign of spellcasting. Not much of a surprise, since a witch had given it to him. But the impression was... off. Unusual. Not like anything he had come across before, and that was saying a lot considering what he'd been exposed to as a detective. But it matched what he had sensed lurking on the other side of the door when talking with the witch.

Giving the door one last distrustful glare, Theo retreated back to the warm safety of his car and gently placed the envelope in the seat beside him.

"Who are you?" Theo asked the envelope sitting innocently, eyeing it warily as if it would grow a mouth and give a snarky answer. The urge to rip open the cream paper was almost enough to move him.

That unexplainable feeling, the instinct that drove him and attributed to every successful investigation he's solved, urged him to find out why the witch was so secretive. Why was she hiding if she was as strong as she seemed?

Curiosity won the short battle, and he reached to snatch up the envelope and tear into the heavy paper. It was part of his job, anyway. He was just being paranoid about things he didn't understand. Slowly, he slid the page out and flipped it right side up to look at it properly.

"What..." He couldn't even finish his thought.

It was a drawing of a woman, deep wrinkles bracketing her mouth as the corners pulled up in a wild smile with a very noticeable beauty mark on the upper lip to the right. Her face was half covered with a black hood from just below the eyes, but there was enough showing to identify the suspect.

But at the same time, it was so much more. It looked to be intricately drawn in charcoal from the blend and smudging he could make out in the dim car light. Like Theo could blink and in the next moment watch the drawing move its mouth and speak in a croaking voice. Along the edges were notes meticulously written in a small, neat hand about a name and aliases, approximate height, hair color, eye color, defining features, a list of addresses he assumed were potential hideouts, and what appeared to be living relatives.

She practically laid this case in his lap. Everything he needed to know was right there on the paper.

But how?

Theo hadn't given her any pertinent details about the suspect. Hell, he didn't even have a suspect when he first pressed that piece of notebook paper against her door. All he had done was describe the location of the crime scene and the victim's appearance. The perspective was from the view of the victim, like it had been Dorianne lying beneath the blade clutched in the bloodied hand dripping viscera from the first stab. The amount of detail was just unreal.

"What the hell..." Theo finally muttered, staring too long into the eyes of the suspect as if he too were her victim. "Who are you, Dorianne Grey?"

Files sat neatly stacked, if not in a haphazard order, across Theo's desk as he spread out the papers of the most recent unauthorized ceremony. Dorianne's art sat right over his keyboard as he studied it and sipped on his third black coffee for the morning.

"Got a report from the trackers," Rebecca said by way of greeting. One hand balanced a plain glazed donut perched on the lid of her usual cinnamon spice latte, while that arm pinched a folder beneath that armpit and the other hand held a backpack thrown over her shoulder. She sauntered in and turned sideways to present the folder to Theo, who barely managed to catch it before she let go and scattered the reports all over the floor. "Good catch, bud."

Theo rolled his eyes. "Can you not start off the morning with a game of pick-up? These reports are hard enough to read when they're in the correct order."

"Sorry, sorry."

"So what did the trackers have to say?" Theo flipped through the pages and pulled the still shots from capture spells the trackers had cast on the crime scene and transferred to paper. Whoever had cast this one did a half-ass job—the images were slightly blurry.

"One of those pages has an index of all the glyphs cataloged on the victim's body," she began, halfway through her first bite of the donut. "Most of them were your average power amplifiers and immobilizers, but there was a string of some kind of runes along his throat the researchers couldn't identify. 'Never seen the likes of them before,' they said."

Theo plucked that particular picture up from inside the file and tried to disconnect his emotions from his job as he examined the body of the victim in high-resolution captures. Very rarely did he come across murders this brutal, even when he was dealing with the run of the mill, no-magic-needed stab and runs in his old life. It churned the breakfast in his stomach thinking about how dismantled the man's poor body had been. Just as she said, there was a line of runes that seemed burned into his skin, black with reddened borders that looked as if they were blistered. He couldn't imagine the man having to sit there, alive, while they did that to his neck.

The more he stared, the more familiar the spiky runes seemed. Where had he seen these before? Certainly not at any crime scene he's been to before now...

His eyes snapped to the drawing Dorianne had given him, scouring every bit of it for clues. Never mind the fact Theo had already spent hours staring at this paper, almost committing it to memory.

"There!"

"Wha—?" Rebecca had been leaning back with her feet propped on the desk and another file in her hand, almost falling back off the chair at his yell. "Warn a lady before you start that! I haven't even started on my coffee, and I almost spilled it!"

"Here!" He indicated excitedly to the small bit of skin just above the hollow of her throat in the drawing. "Look! On her neck, in exactly the same spot! Doesn't this look similar to the victim?" He passed it over the desks when she threw down her own report to take the drawing from him. Her eyes flitted over it in a meticulous manner. Rebecca was very familiar with how Dorianne delivered her information.

Absently, she shoved the rest of the donut into her mouth and brushed the crumbs off on her pants. "Did you just pick this up from D last night?"

"D? Oh, from Dorianne, yes." He had been caught off-guard with the nickname Rebecca had revealed. D... he thought that was a little too casual to use for a powerful witch. But that lack-of-formality vibe was par for the course for Rebecca.

"Here," she pointed at a specific part of the chain of runes where the carotid artery would be, "is this rune in the exact same spot on the victim?"

Theo scrambled to find the crime scene picture again. They laid the two side-by-side, both turned so they could look at them together.

"Yeah." Theo's finger pointed to the same spot on the man. "Look here. Do you think that's what actually kills the person who wears these runes? Why the hell would the woman doing the killing have a spell like this on her throat too?"

Rebecca stared at the woman's portrait, but her gaze was a mile away. "Maybe it's insurance."

That baffled Theo. "Insurance for what?"

"You see on the victim? Those runes were branded into his neck probably shortly after he was captured. They're very deep and the skin around them is irritated and blistering like it just happened. But on the suspect, they at least look healed. This person is probably not the leader, but whoever put these on her might use it like a collar, you know? How else would someone control a witch like this?"

The theory held water. "So... this woman killed the victim because she was being controlled?"

"Oh, hell no!" Rebecca leaned back and crossed her arms. An angry scowl darkened her face. "She knew exactly what she was doing, and it was for wholly selfish reasons. The amount of amplification runes and power spells on that poor guy was enough to paint the picture she was trying to steal his very considerable power. His family is well-known for being strong earth pact-bearers. No... that spell on her throat is meant to keep her in check. Keep her from getting *too* powerful. At least, that's my guess."

They sat together in mutually-agreed silence, chewing on the evidence laid out in front of them. Theo didn't know much about the inner workings of a coven, obviously, but what kind of leader does this to its members? If there is a constant threat of getting too strong, what even is the point of these magic-stealing rituals?

The deeper they dove into this case, the more murky the waters seemed.

Theo needed to find the suspect, that much was plain to him. But did he point out to Rebecca the similarity of those runes on the suspect and victim's necks to the ones etched on Dorianne's door? He couldn't outright interrogate the SIA's pet witch... but he could interrogate the suspect with no repercussions from the captain. He'd be doing his job.

He swiped up the pictures and jammed them back into the file in a rush. That level of carelessness was atypical for him, but Theo hoped his short-term partner wouldn't notice that.

"I'll make you a copy and leave it on the desk." He tried not to sound as rushed as he felt. "I have some parts of the report to file with the tracking unit now that I have the drawing. Catch up later."

Theo hoped that was excuse enough to escape Rebecca's watchful eye, and he snatched his jacket off the back of his chair to dash out.

Chapter Three

There are a lot of things Theo had encountered in his short time at the SIA, and much more with his time in the non-magic side of law enforcement. Not everyone was a power-hungry witch performing unsanctioned rituals, after all. There were plenty of humans just like Theo, not well-versed in spellcasting but still a victim of the green-eyed monster, and therefore enticed to commit criminal acts.

He didn't, however, expect to pull up in front of a—dare he say, cute—white house in a quiet suburb of Salem, trimmed in light pink with a red door. Theo double checked the address to the one written in Dorianne's neat hand above the suspect's portrait. It was the same.

The lawn was perfectly maintained, a white picket fence lining it, and some children's toys laid scattered about the grass like they had been called in, mid-play. His thoughts strayed to Dorianne's equally-unassuming brownstone. Those witches certainly knew how to put up innocent fronts.

Theo pulled his car into the smooth driveway. The longer he spent looking at the house, the more suspicious it seemed. It was *too* perfect. Compared to the older-looking houses in the neighborhood, this one looked brand new. The concrete all around it was without a single crack. None of the lights were on. Even with the abundance of toys laying around, there was nothing but silence coming from the house. He didn't really know much about kids, but he knew they got loud and filthy.

This house felt... hollow.

An uneasy feeling settled heavily in Theo's stomach. The same feeling that told him he was about to get his ass handed to him on a stakeout, or get ambushed at a scene. He attributed far too many close calls to that gut feeling. His hand shifted to the pistol at his side, armed with some magic-nullifying bullets the SIA research team developed. Theo never used them before to verify their claims, and he hoped he wouldn't have to.

He left the car and shut the door gently, trying to act casual to not alert the neighbors who may be curious, or even worse, lookouts. He climbed the porch with a little hop in his step and, when reaching the door, noticed the ever-so-faint etchings along the frame. Whoever had put them there did so painstakingly, blending the runes into the grain of the wood so as to appear natural, as if they were just small blemishes in the whorls.

Now Theo's suspicions were confirmed. A witch lived in this house, or at least used it to hide. Upon closer inspection of the frame, one particular line right at eye level had his blood running cold. Immediately, he pulled the null-gun from its holster and held it with both hands.

There were death runes on this house. Just like the Dorianne's. Just like around the victim's throat. And just like the wall in his house when his parents were murdered. They were all connected somehow, this murderous cult with their fucked-up ceremonies and Dorianne, who the agency relied so heavily on to sniff these witches out.

The sudden spike of rage that blasted through his common sense urged Theo to just kick the door down and go in, gun blazing. His teeth ground with how tightly he clenched his jaw. The grip of the pistol would probably be imprinted in his palm for hours with how tightly he clutched it.

"Motherfuckers," he hissed as softly as he could. Now trying to keep the porch floorboards from creaking under his shoes, he moved over to the edge of the closest window to his right and tried to peek through any crack in the lacy white drapes. A sheer, but obvious, layer of distortion wavered over the inside of the glass, shifting colors like oil spilled on water.

The windows had been warded to deter peeking.

He stepped back, eyeing the house skeptically, when a flash of something dark caught the corner of his eye from the edge of the porch. Something that was moving around the side of the house toward the back.

"Shit!" he spat angrily and darted to the railing, vaulting over the banister to land uneasily on the paved driveway that extended all the way to a shed in the backyard. Wet footprints that had not been there before zigzagged across the pavement, as if the owner was staggering. Like maybe someone who had just performed a very draining ceremony and hadn't recovered yet.

The person stumbled over the bricks lining the driveway in an effort to get up the back porch stairs, gripping the handrail to stop their fall. It bought Theo just enough time to sprint closer and catch the person by their shoulder and rip them off. They both tumbled painfully to the ground in a heap of thrown elbows and angry words spat at each other.

From his very limited vantage point, Theo assumed the person was a woman, judging from the nails digging into his biceps and high-pitched screeches. Her face was partially covered by a black pullover, the hood not quite thrown off her head yet. But the bottom of her face that was visible was enough. The beauty mark at the corner of her mouth and lips thinning with age was identical to the drawing Dorianne had given him.

"Stop moving!" Theo commanded the flailing witch. "Under the Practitioner Monitoring Act, you are to remain silent with your hands by your head and are explicitly forbidden from casting—"

"Fuck you!"

The woman was practically feral. One of her hands reached for something in her pocket so quickly he couldn't catch it, and with a bitter scream slammed it into his right side with all her strength. What felt like a blade slid between his ribs before she snapped off the grip and tossed it away.

Immediately the right side of his torso went numb and cold, so his right arm that held the gun fell limp. The gun buried itself in the tall grass, and the witch tried to twist and flip over to grab it. Theo was barely quick enough to dive over and snatch it up—along with a handful of grass—and swing the muzzle around to point at her head. The move shifted his weight just enough to let her buck him off and send them both sprawling in opposite directions.

"*Stop!*"

The hood had slid off completely from the witch's head, exposing knotted gray hair that fell into bloodshot eyes. Wide with wild aggression, they were a fantastic combination of green with a noticeable starburst of gold around the irises. She crouched to a defensive position, hands outstretched but palms facing the ground.

The grass around him sharpened and lengthened to literal blades jutting from the ground as if stabbed by the earth itself. Theo narrowly avoided being skewered through the calves, but collected some severe gashes as he threw himself from the circle of green daggers that shuddered and retracted back into the ground. His shoulder complained painfully as he landed on a softer patch of grass, but immediately realized his mistake as the witch moved her downturn hands in his direction again. He rolled himself over and got to his feet to jump onto the lowest step of the back porch as more blades shot up at him.

"This is getting old, witch! You're only making things worse by attacking an SIA agent!"

It was obvious she didn't give a shit who he was or where he was from. The thorn bushes planted by the porch lashed out with barbed whips, one of which caught him across the chest and thrashed, ripping flesh through his jacket and button-up and leaving behind a tattered mess. Another vine darted to pin Theo's left wrist to the floor so he couldn't lift his gun and dug in thorns half as long as his pinky finger. The excruciating pain and grating feeling as they rubbed something in his wrist hinted at hitting bone, but he hoped that wasn't the case.

"Mother of..." he spat and scrambled back, pinning his back against the house and pushing himself up with his legs alone while fighting against the unbelievable strength of the vine holding him. The right side of his body throbbed from the injury on his side, still cold but just a little less numb and immobile. His fingers twitched madly. "Laurel Greene, cease all magic casting or I will shoot!"

He may not hit her on the first shot, but he would still shoot.

Her lips pulled back, revealing decayed black teeth clenched together and a small dribble of blood that leaked from between them. Something was severely wrong with her, maybe even to the point it was killing her.

"Our roots run deep, fool! Killing one sprout will hardly make a difference to the coven!"

A building pressure weighted the air between them, thick with powerful magic waiting to be commanded. Theo gritted his teeth against the excruciating pain shooting across his chest and around his wrist as he tried to lift the gun in his left hand faster than she could cast.

His finger pulled the hair trigger.

BANG!

Blue fire burst from the muzzle as the bullet shot from its barrel, kicking his shoulder back painfully.

But he was a heartbeat too late.

Her body twisted with the impact to her right shoulder, throwing the witch to the ground when the null-magic bullet hit true. The head, however, fell with a sickening *thud* almost exactly where she had been standing just a second before. It rocked slightly, her face twisted in a grotesque death mask. The foliage around them immediately drooped and shriveled away without her magic to control them.

Theo could hardly process what just happened. "What the actual fuck?" He shoved himself slowly from where he was braced against the house and stumbled down the steps. His legs gave out and he fell to his knees beside the witch's decapitated head.

Ringing her pale throat like an intricate choker were black runes, neatly cut in half where it seemed to have been sliced from her body with a sharp blade. A blade she didn't have in either hand. And a blade she wouldn't have been able to conceal until now that was long enough to cleave a head from its body. Even with only half the symbols there, Theo knew what kind of runes they were. The same runes that keep popping up every time he deals with this coven. Or with Dorianne.

Death runes.

She—or whoever had control of the spell those runes activated—had killed her just before his bullet hit. How quickly it was cast blew his mind. Or the purpose behind it.

"Well, shit," Theo cursed quietly as his gaze drifted across her cooling corpse. Before his very eyes, the body blackened and disintegrated, falling apart like charred logs in a fire.

No body, no suspect, and no new answers to any of the questions clogging his mind from thinking clearly.

"This is gonna be a bitch to put in a report."

Hobbling to his desk the next morning proved to be an excruciating exercise in conviction. Theo gripped his right side and lowered himself into the chair with a pained hiss. He only hoped…

"What the hell happened to you?"

Shit.

He did not have the mental capacity to deal with Rebecca this morning. He felt feverish and shaky and hungover all at once. His own misplaced sense of pride was the only thing that had stopped him from calling in to work sick this morning. Now he wished he had.

Perfect attendance was not worth being berated by his mother hen of a partner.

The smirk that had lit her face fell quickly as she took in his bedraggled appearance. "Wow, I was mostly kidding, but you really look like death. What are you even doing here, trying to spread a plague? Get outta here!"

"I'm fine," Theo muttered, lifting his hand weakly to wave over the screen and wake up his computer. The screen flickered in an attempt to come to life before fading to black again.

Now she was scowling. "You're definitely *not* okay. Your aura is all over the place. Like a..." Theo could see the pieces fall into place behind her chocolate eyes. "Did you mess with a witch? That looks like a nasty curse."

"Curses only work on magic users. I don't use it."

"That doesn't mean you don't have magic, Theo." Her tone was very no-nonsense and she stalked around the desk to get a closer look at him. "Actually, I would argue you are a very strong tracker, if you ever put the effort into training." Rebecca's observant gaze zeroed in on the side he had been stabbed. "Are you... is that blood?"

He touched the area between his ribs where it hurt the most, and pulled away bloody fingertips tinged with an odd black substance streaking through the red. Rebecca dropped to her knees and gripped the front of his plain blue button-down, ripping it open and sending buttons skittering across the floor.

"Hey, watch it, Reb—"

Her shaky exhale stopped his protesting. The sheer look of fear and worry that had dropped across her face was a blast of frigid wind that had him instantly on alert, the groggy fog in his head blown away. With a shaking hand, Rebecca lightly grazed the angry skin around the stab wound.

It looked disgustingly infected, black veins spreading out in a webbed pattern across his ribs. Dark red blood seeped through the bandage he slapped over it before leaving the flat that morning.

"It wasn't doing that when I left..." Theo's excuse seemed pathetic, even to his own ears. His head felt like it had been stuffed with cotton since he woke up. He hardly remembered how he got to the office and only vaguely remembered locking his condo.

"Because your body is trying to reject the curse." She pointed to the black streaks across his tanned skin. "It's probably reacting to the anti-curse wards placed on the headquarters. Why the alarms didn't go off is..."

"Not good?"

Rebecca leveled a dark glare on him, probably the most serious Theo had ever seen her in the few months they had been partnered. "No, idiot, not good at all! Who did this to you?"

"Er..." He rubbed the back of his neck nervously and looked away to the far wall beyond her angry face. "Just a witch, like you said."

"This isn't your normal 'you pissed me off' kind of curse. Whoever did this put a lot of effort into creating it specifically for..." True fear, completely out of place on her usually happy-go-lucky face, sent a reciprocal bolt shooting through him. "You need to get the hell out of here, *now*!"

"What? No, we have the case—"

"For once listen to me, dumbass," she hissed angrily, snatching his backpack and her own briefcase up before jerking him to shaky legs with a grip twisted into the shoulder of his ragged shirt. The aggressiveness of her voice was so out of character for Rebecca it lit a fire under his ass. "Put your jacket on over that mess and button it up. Hurry!"

He didn't have the fight in him to argue with her. It took an embarrassing amount of time—and a lot of creative expletives—to get his arms into their sleeves and the jacket buttoned up to hide the bloody injury. By now it was throbbing a steady rhythm that almost seemed to match his heartbeat, a pain stabbing into his side with every pulse. Rebecca was at the door to their office, peering down either end of the hallway.

"Come on." She gestured with the wave of a hand, still not looking at him as she darted out and made her way down to the elevator. Surely, she was looking out for the Captain.

Theo shuddered to think how that situation would pan out, running into him in this state.

He made it all the way to the doors Rebecca held open with a foot braced against one side and hobbled inside, when a booming voice came down the hall and made them both jump nervously.

"Rebecca!" the Captain called. "Do you have a minute? I have the code for those files you asked about... Hey, are you alright?"

"Sure, Cap! I'm fine, why?"

"Uh... who's tracking blood on the floor then?"

Theo and Rebecca both snapped their heads down to the floor, and Theo cursed violently. He had indeed left a little spattered trail from the office all the way to the elevator. How his side had progressed this quickly to a bleeding mess terrified him. Theo's breath sawed in and out as his vision wavered.

"Er, just stabbed myself with a letter opener!" Her lie came easily and she jammed a hand into her pocket, the one out of Captain's direct line of sight. "I was heading to the medic to grab a bandage. Sorry for making such a mess!"

She reached in and felt around for the first floor button and jabbed it aggressively. "Oops, sorry, gotta go, or I'll bleed out in the elevator!

I'll catch up later, Captain!" Her completely insincere apology was cut off with the elevator doors shutting just as the captain's face appeared, the most confused expression on his strong face.

Theo sagged against the elevator wall. A sheen of sweat glistened on his face, skin now ghastly pale. Rebecca turned to look at him and her concerned frown was not comforting in the least.

"Wow, you really look like crap now."

He huffed, Theo's humor squashed. "Thanks, partner."

Every moment stuck in that metal box felt like an eternity, Theo slowly leaking onto the laminate tile and Rebecca scrutinizing him with a hawk-like eye. The cheery music playing over the small speakers was extremely offensive given the circumstance. So was the innocent chime indicating they reached the first floor.

Rebecca grabbed his arm with a firm but gentle hand and pulled Theo toward the door leading out to the main thoroughfare in front of the SIA headquarters. She angled her body to block his bloodied side from the security desk they had to pass on the way out. Even so, curious eyes followed their hurried dash across the main foyer.

"Where are we going?" Theo finally had the audacity to ask.

"My place."

"Via?"

She shot him a loaded side-eye and pulled him toward the crosswalk, punching the button multiple times to let them cross the busy road.

"Considering you're possibly a ticking time bomb for whatever curse you managed to get stabbed with, we will have to take my car. And you bet your sweet cheeks that I'm sending you the cleaning bill for the mess I'm sure you will make in it."

Unfortunately, the parking lot was still a short hike away from the SIA building.

"You couldn't pull the car around for me?" He grouched miserably. "I'm kind of bleeding out here."

"Judging from your ability to gripe about it, you're not that close to death yet." She threw his right arm over her shoulder to take some of his weight, carelessly pushing against the bloody mess to help him stay upright for the slow trek to her small car. "And don't think you've gotten out of telling me exactly how you got this little jab, eh?"

Theo groaned loudly, either from the pain in his side or the idea of admitting his failure in capturing the dark witch. Both felt unpleasant, to say the least.

As they drew closer to the nondescript black car issued by the SIA, the locks clicked open automatically with a concentrated thought from Rebecca. The passenger door popped open for her to pull and gently lower Theo into the bucket seat. Theo's head fell back against the seat, winded and sweating profusely now.

She looked over him with concern. "Are you going to die in my car? I need to know before I start driving."

Theo snorted, then winced at the stabbing pain. "I hope not. I would hate to rob you of berating me for the next hour by dying a silent death on the way."

Her eyes rolled. "Yep, sarcasm is still intact at least."

"That will be the last to go."

Chapter Four

Theo thanked whatever divine entity watching over him that Rebecca's apartment had an elevator. He didn't think he could survive stairs.

Rebecca swung them into an underground parking garage and into the assigned parking spot for her unit, 4D. Strangely, he never had the opportunity to come over to her place despite her open personality and motherly instincts. Then again, he never really pushed for an invitation or reciprocated with one to his place, either.

"Think you can make it to the elevator?" Rebecca unlatched their belts and opened the doors. "It looks like the bleeding has already slowed down. How are you feeling?"

"Like I've been bleeding out in your car."

"Ha ha. Get out, punk."

Despite the playful banter, she reached in carefully and helped Theo to his feet, steadying him when he wavered slightly on unsteady legs and braced a hand on the roof of the car. She slung his arm over her shoulder again and moved at his slower pace to the waiting lift. There was a blank space beside the door, a rectangular shape surrounded by tiny runes etched into the wall. It vaguely reminded him of the consultant's door. Rebecca placed her hand against the wall within the runes, and they pulsed a faint yellow before the elevator lurched upward.

"You do realize now that I have you here, you're not leaving until you tell me everything, right?"

He sighed. "I figured that's what you really brought me here for, not because you actually cared for my well-being."

"Has anyone told you how cheeky you've gotten?"

"Only because I have to hang out with you regularly."

Her booming laugh filled the elevator as they both rested against the plain wood-paneled wall. "My God, I've created a monster!"

Not that he was expecting Rebecca to baby him, but her overly-casual response to him bleeding profusely all over her was slightly disconcerting. "Please tell me you at least have some bandages at your place. I'm not sure I could make it through an interrogation like this."

"Even better." She lifted her hands and wiggled her fingers like she was showing a magic trick. "I'll fix you up myself. Well, sort of. Can't guarantee it will be pleasant, but you'll live."

"Great." He didn't feel great at all.

The elevator opened directly into a small foyer, neatly kept with a coat rack beside the elevator door and shoes in an orderly row to the left. A small table held a crystal bowl Rebecca emptied her pockets into, throwing the wallet that held her SIA badge and the car fob into it before coming back to help Theo out.

"Honey, I'm home!" she called cheerfully into the condo.

"Hi, babe! I'm in the kitchen!" an airy, bubbly voice called from deeper in the house. The clanking of pots and running water punctuated her response as the person bustled around in a kitchen. Rebecca led Theo to one of the chairs in the quaint dining room, making sure he was settled before following the voice into what he assumed was the kitchen attached to it. Rebecca growled playfully and a girlish giggle answered her as the pots clattered about some more, followed by the definite sounds of some very animated kissing.

"What's for lunch, love?"

"Uh, what makes you think I made anything?" the woman answered in a coquettish voice. Then there was more laughter as Rebecca did something to her that involved more growls and lowly muttered words.

"Why are—" A tall, thin woman walked through the open doorway to the dining room, her gaze immediately landing on Theo's slumping form at the dining table. "Rebecca Ann Yarrow, what the hell are you doing leaving your poor partner like this?"

The woman flitted over to him and light hands brushed over him, pushing back the hair that had fallen over his forehead and patting his cheek in a dotting fashion. "Are you okay, dear?"

"He's fine." Rebecca appeared in the kitchen doorway, a glass of red wine swirled in a stemmed glass held lightly in her hand. "I figured you could fix him up, Dylan, my love?"

So this was Dylan.

Theo had heard about Rebecca's romantic partner in passing, but this was certainly not what—or who—he was expecting. All he knew of her marital history was that her deceased husband was also in the

SIA many years ago and they had started as partners, before she became a handler. He died in the line of duty, and that was all she said about it. He heard Rebecca call Dylan by name and just assumed she was with another man.

He certainly didn't imagine this slip of a woman, all dark chocolatey hair spilling out of a thick braid over her shoulder and round, doll-like eyes with such a heavy shatter-pattern the green of her irises were little more than slivers between the black cracks expanding out from her pupils and giving Dylan away as an extremely powerful practitioner. Those eyes instantly put Theo on edge. She seemed way too docile to put up with someone as abrupt as Rebecca.

"Oh, honey!" Dylan continued to poke and prod Theo, pulling off his jacket to inspect the scrapes and cuts along his arms. "We'll get you all sorted out, then we can sit down to some chicken pot pie."

This whole experience was disconcerting to Theo. Most of his childhood was bouncing from foster home to foster home, none of them worried about the cuts and scrapes he got from scuffling at school or feeding him chicken pot pie. Just a few minutes in Dylan's presence hinted at that long-lost feeling of a doting mother he had robbed from him.

She bustled off to another part of the condo, a flurry of pink skirt swirling around pale legs, leaving him alone with Rebecca as she continued to sip from her glass. "You didn't mention Dylan was a woman."

"You didn't ask," she replied instantly. "And, does it really matter?"

"Not at all. I'm just shocked an over-sharer such as yourself wouldn't disclose something like that."

She shrugged. "She makes me happy. And that's all that matters."

"Fair enough. Also, isn't it a bit early to drink wine? It's not even noon yet."

Rebecca gave the glass a thoughtful look, then shrugged and downed another hearty mouthful. Dylan bustled back in with a small wooden box, sitting in the chair beside him as she pulled out bandages and various jars. Intricate runes crawled across the lid and pulsed a soft green when her hand touched the side of it.

"I am a pact-bearer with earth magic, so I should be able to fix you up in a jiffy!"

This intrigued Theo. "So, can you make plants grow and things like that?"

"That's the most basic skill we learn, yes, but I specialize more in healing."

"Huh..." he muttered absently. "The witch I ran into was able to make the grass grow knife-like blades and crazy thorn whips with vines. Is that the same kind of magic too?"

Dylan shrugged as she dabbed some opaque white paste on some of the smaller cuts along the tops of his hands he hadn't bothered treating. "It depends on the pact she made. Magic is extremely transactional, but one must have an affinity with a particular type to be able to make a pact. People who don't have an affinity usually have varying degrees of sensitivity to magic being used and become trackers in some capacity."

"Like the ones at SIA?"

"Most law enforcement are on the spectrum of trackers, I would imagine. Even if they don't practice spells openly, magic can manifest in strong senses or intuition that help them with investigations."

"His right side is the worst, babe." Rebecca gestured from the kitchen door with her full wine glass. Her casual lean with a shoulder against the door frame was a far cry from the urgency she showed just an hour before at headquarters. Clearly, she trusted Dylan's healing magic. "Apparently, he decided to take on a witch. On his own. Without telling me—"

"Fine, we get it, you're pissed. Can we drop it now?" Theo grumbled while unbuttoning his ruined shirt.

She raised her glass to him. "I'm fine now. Obviously."

"Good luck getting her to let anything go," Dylan confirmed his fears. "She still won't forgive me for the time I accidentally gave her food poisoning with some cupcakes I baked."

"I forgave you. I just won't forget. Hence the reason you are not allowed to bake anymore."

Dylan rolled her eyes, pulling on Theo's shoulder to turn his injured side closer to her. Whatever she saw made her forehead crinkle in concern, poking and pulling at his skin to get a better look at the stab wound. "You said the witch made plants attack you? And stabbed you with a knife?"

"Yeah," he grimaced, hissing in pain as she continued her exam. "I thought something broke off when she stabbed me, but I couldn't find anything in there when I went home to doctor it. But it's been throbbing and bleeding a little since last night. It only turned this nasty black color and felt worse when I went to work this morning. Think I need stitches, doc?"

She snorted. "Don't give me that kind of liability. If you die, Rebecca is one hundred percent in charge of getting rid of your body."

"Gladly."

Theo threw his partner a dark glare.

"Well," Dylan leaned back, arms crossed as she continued to peruse his injury, "I don't see anything in the cut now, so that's good news. As to why it's acting like this... if she was an earth pact-bearer, it could be poison. The dark ones have a tendency to come up with some particularly nasty concoctions. I'll take some samples to test and make some poultices to put on it, and in a couple days see how it looks. I'm hesitant to stitch it if she did poison you and your body is trying to flush it out. Given that you're not dead yet and there isn't any kind of branching from the wound, it will probably clear up in the next couple of days."

"Really? I could have sworn it looked worse." His head craned down to get a look at it. "It was bleeding like crazy and burning at the office."

"Hmmm..." Dylan bent down to look at it again. "It looks fine now. I mean, as fine as a day-old stab wound can look. But my unprofessional opinion is that whatever she stabbed you with was more of a defensive counter than intent to kill."

"Thanks, babe." Rebecca swept into the room, carrying a second glass of wine to set by her elbow. Dylan obviously had the same opinion as Theo about being too early for it as she shot Rebecca a questioning look. She left it untouched as she plucked supplies off the table to place neatly back into the box.

"I only did it so you wouldn't have to spend the day in Tate's office explaining why your partner is dead," she teased, tilting her head up to receive the kiss Rebecca pecked on her lips. She rose gracefully and pat Theo on the head like he was a child. "Try to stay out of trouble, Theo? You seem like a good guy, and Rebecca would be very sad to have anything happen to you."

Something about her slightly condescending tone rankled him. Theo tried to not get offended; surely, he was just in a bad mood from being stabbed. There was something about her magic, too, that he couldn't put his finger on but sent goosebumps running along his skin wherever Dylan touched. The same oppressive pressure he felt standing in front of Dorianne's home filled the room, but it was more of a gentle press than an overwhelming force.

"Do you belong to a coven?"

Immediately, Dylan's shoulders stiffened as her head bowed over the contents of the box she busied herself with. If he hadn't been watching her face so intently, the fiendish smirk would have come and gone without him ever knowing. A darkness shuttered her naturally bright eyes that gave a particularly sinister look to her otherwise innocent-looking features. Rebecca had wandered back into the kitchen and the distinct clanging of bottles indicated she was probably refilling her wine, so she missed her partner's odd reaction to the question.

"I do. And in a particularly high rank, if you're wondering."

He wasn't. Neither was his surprised, given what he saw from the shatter-pattern in her eyes.

Theo was curious to know *which* coven it was, considering there were not many in the area courtesy of the Black Staff. Even less so a coven of earth magic practitioners. She didn't seem open to indulging more questions as she swept the remaining bits of her healing items off the edge of the table and into the box without the tediousness from a few minutes earlier, snapping the lid shut with a definitive *tap*. The abrupt change to such an icy demeanor was interesting, to say the least.

Just like she came, Dylan whisked away in a flurry of skirts and fluttering hair to somewhere else in their spacious apartment, taking her wooden box with her.

She brushed past Rebecca without a second look, leaving her slightly bewildered as she watched her partner retreat to their bedroom and shut the door. She thought it odd Dylan would run off so quickly—usually she was excited and chatty when the occasional visitor came over. Rebecca made a mental note to check on her after tying things up with Theo.

Rebecca took her seat and leaned back, one hand tucked under the other elbow as she brought the wine up to her lips. "So, care to explain how and why you were at a witch's house by yourself? You know, brainstorming for the book-length report you're gonna have to turn into the captain."

Theo groaned and reached for his own glass of water. "Can we not with the snarky questions? I've kinda had a shit day if you couldn't already tell."

"Fair. But what in the actual hardboiled fuck did you think you were gonna do against a magic user? And a dark one, at that. You know, one that doesn't care about the laws or that she would have a body to deal with later."

"First of all, I wasn't planning to run into her," Theo replied gruffly. "I just went to one of the possible locations on the consultant's drawing, just to see how accurate her freaky magic really was."

Rebecca's brow furrowed. "Again, you didn't think to call that in to me?"

He bypassed the question entirely. "So... how do I deal with the coven if I don't have my own... whoo whoo–" Theo waggled his fingers in Rebecca's direction. She raised an eyebrow, unimpressed at his choice of words. "Or whatever kind of magic they have? They didn't really prepare us for this in the academy beyond target practice with the null guns. Which are, by the way, a bitch to shoot one-handed."

"Of course they didn't." She rolled her eyes and took another swig of wine. "At the risk of sounding old, they really are doing a disservice to kids these days. Especially the trackers..." Rebecca lifted her hips to reach for the back pocket of her pants, where she procured the notebook she usually uses at crime scenes. From an inner pocket she pulled a fountain pen.

"You seriously carry around a fountain pen—"

"Focus," she snapped, ripping some pages out of the notebook and tossing the rest of the book on the table before pulling the cap off her fancy pen. "M'kay, so you know there's two main types of magic that we've managed to identify through research run by the SIA, right? Please tell me they at least went over that in onboarding."

Theo grumbled. "Yes, but—"

"So there are pact-bearers, the ones who cast magic," she barreled through his response, busy drawing a t-chart to emphasize her point. "And there are the trackers, who are mostly just good at sensing magic and can, depending on their individual skills, cast magic related to tracking its use, hence their name."

He sighed, exasperated, and rested his chin in his hand as he propped his elbow on the table. From Rebecca's long-winded explanations when he first started as her partner, he knew to brace for the long haul.

Rebecca continued to fill in the chart, with pact-bearers on the left and trackers on the right. "The difference between their magic is that pact-bearers perform a ritual to unlock their power, so to speak. Like opening a channel. But then you have dark witches," she drew a circle completely separate from the chart, "who think they can run roughshod over the natural order of things and try to push the boundaries of their magic by performing sacrificial rituals, magic gets out of control quickly when elements of death are involved."

"Why is that?"

"Well..." The end of the pen tapped against the table methodically. "It's really only speculation, since the Restoration Era seems to be when humans gained the ability to use magic starting some two hundred years ago. Most of that time we've spent bumbling about, trying to gain back everything we lost as a society. But the theory is that every magical element humans can harness has a natural counterpart, something that stops or at least slows it down. A check and balance.

"But death is unstoppable, unmovable. So when someone starts dickin' around with the natural order by forcing something like that into their rituals, magic starts to become unstable and unpredictable. Rule number one of magic casting is, don't fuck with the natural order. Hence the reason the SIA exists."

"Uh huh... so what about our witch friend? What category does Dorianne fall in on your little chart?"

She heaved a weary sigh, leaning back in her chair and tossing the pen to the table on top of her notes. "She is... a total mystery. She has to be some kind of pact-bearer to be able to use magic to the extent she does, but no one—not even the big brains at SIA research—can figure out what bucket she falls into. Even under the broad elements of earth, fire, wind, and water, she doesn't seem to be specialized in any singular one like a normal pact-bearer would. Maybe the closest would be shadow magic, since she may be sensitive to sunlight? But no one has ever displayed abilities dealing solely with shadows. That's deep in the dark spectrum, and with all we know, no one deals in dark magic alone. At least, no one who wants to keep their life does."

"Because they would be making a pact with shadows?" Theo was trying to wrap his head around the inner workings of witches. He felt particularly stupid for not really paying attention to this side of humanity, considering he used a minimal amount of magic every day, turning on lights or starting his car. It was just what he grew up with. He had no recollection of his parents being magic users.

"No. A witch like that would be making a pact with Death itself."

Just the thought sent chills down his spine. Theo straightened from his slump with a pained hiss, hungry for any kind of insight to the mysterious woman on the other side of that door. The door that was guarded with death runes.

How deep was she involved in that kind of magic?

Just how far did her power reach?

It seemed Theo had received the necessary care and instruction, after Rebecca forced him to stay for lunch and kept an eye on him long enough to assuage her fear of him bleeding out again. Dylan still hadn't come out from their bedroom by the time Rebecca offered him a ride back to his house. She hadn't turned on the light, either, from what they could tell from the darkness beneath the door. Whatever had her all twisted up made Rebecca uneasy.

"I couldn't in good conscience send you home with an empty stomach and a hole in your side," she had declared. He barely got through the heaping pile of chicken pot pie she plopped onto his plate. How getting overfed helped him in any way was still a mystery. "I'll have Dylan give me a ride to pick up your car and drop it off later."

It was probably better for his psyche staying for lunch than sitting at his counter—alone—with a double whiskey after getting his ass kicked.

The snippets he had gleaned about Dorianne hardly scratched the surface of answers his mind required for a moment of peace, though. If it was so bad to be fucking around with death magic, why were those same runes on his living room wall as they were on the door frames of two witches? He had assumed whoever killed his parents had written them on the walls as a warning. Realizing now how much power the runes had, surely that would have been a process that yielded some kind of measurable result. Detectives that inspected the scene of his parents' death up declared the area completely magic-free. Nothing had been casted that they could detect.

At least, nothing successful had been casted.

Were his parents responsible for scrawling those foreboding runes on the wall? Was that what took their life, a moment of desperation trying to protect him from whoever came banging on the door that night? Maybe that spell did exactly what it was supposed to do, and took their lives in exchange. How would the detectives have known that, looking at some archaic runes like those?

There was yet another connection between the murderous cult and his past, and to the SIA's witch consultant.

Theo, caught up in his own head as the undercurrents of questions pulled him deeper and deeper, dinner was a foregone conclusion. Showering was more of a wet towel wipe-down, he was so covered with bandages and medicine Dylan had smeared over his numerous cuts and scrapes. After pulling on a loose pair of sweatpants, Theo hobbled over and tossed himself on the neatly made bed, throwing an arm over his eyes in a sad attempt to flip the switch on his overactive imagination. Even lying down, his injured side throbbed, not as painful as before but a constant reminder of his mistake.

"Fucking witches," he grumbled and jerked the top sheet out from under his body, settling in for another restless night.

Chapter Five

Golden rays from the morning sun had barely made it through Theo's bedroom window before the incessant vibration of his scrying compact pulled him from fitful sleep. He wasn't much of a cheerful person on the best days. Uncaffeinated and recovering from a vicious stab wound, he was an entirely different menace to anyone unfortunate enough to interact with him.

"Slater." His voice was more of a growl as he shook off the remnants of a fitful sleep. He didn't give a damn who was on the other end of the mirror. This was his first day off in the last two years—not that it was entirely voluntary—and he was trying to make the best of it with a morning sleeping in.

"Good morning, Theo."

Hearing Captain Killian Tate's low voice made Theo want to fling himself back onto his bed. Nothing good ever came from a wake-up call from him. The tone of his voice was off from the gruff bark he usually used, though.

Shit. There's been another ritual. Fucking perfect.

"Sir." Theo's tone was more respectful, if only a little. Still, his arm was flung over his eyes as the compact sat cracked open beside his head on the pillow. "To what do I owe this call?"

"I have bad news."

Oh, shit. Theo's mind snapped to full awareness now. His thoughts immediately swung to the other end of the pessimistic spectrum, worried this call was more of a 'don't come back' after all. *I'm getting fired. Rebecca told Tate all about me going off the leash and now I will have to open a private investigation shop just to—*

"Rebecca was found this morning."

A light breeze swept through the birch tree outside his window, the branches scraping lightly against the wood planking. Someone's dog barked from the next street over. Theo's MAED gave a happy chirp as it left its docking station and proceeded to make coffee in the kitchen. And Theo's pulse beat so loud in his ears, it almost drowned out everything.

All these mundane noises were offensive in light of what the captain uttered in what Theo now realized was a mournful, bleak voice. In his line of work, he didn't get calls when people were "found" still breathing. Especially not from the captain.

"Where?"

His body was moving on its own, shoving off the edge of his bed and opening the closet door, leaving the innocuous gold compact sitting on the bed. He grabbed whatever button-up his hands touched without really looking to see what it was and whipped it around to push his arms through. The chances he even buttoned up the shirt properly were very slim before stepping into a pair of black slacks.

"About four miles northwest of the last scene, the one you two were sent to last week. The dispatcher already sent a preliminary tracker team out to—"

"I'm going."

Rage was too simple a name for the emotions roiling in his chest and squeezing his throat in an unforgiving grip. Theo hadn't known Rebecca much longer than his short training period to take over her role, but she managed to worm her way through the cracks in the wall he'd built to keep everyone out since childhood. Yesterday, she had been happily chatting about her grandson's birthday gift on the drive back to his house, a bear she had enchanted to talk with her voice. Her youngest daughter was getting married in the summer.

Rebecca Yarrow was an integral part of so many lives, both in her family and at SIA. To hear she was gone was... unreal. The gaping hole she left behind grew by the minute as Theo realized everyone she had affected with her warm, motherly presence. Even at headquarters, she always remembered everyone's birthday and wished them well. She made them feel welcome. Just like she had made him feel welcome when Theo was suddenly thrust into the world of practitioner investigation.

"... Theo?" He had no idea what Captain Tate had said for the last two minutes he'd been staring off at his white wall. "You still there, son?"

Theo kicked himself back into action. "Will you send over the preliminary findings?"

"You're too close to this, Slater. I mostly called as a courtesy before you walked into the office and found out. Let the trackers take this—"

"Don't we need the witch to give us a suspect profile?"

Killian's tense silence was answer enough.

I had to keep my personal shit out of this if the SIA was going to use the consultant.

Whatever spellcasting she used to glean that information to find the witch that stabbed him, Theo needed if he wanted any chance of finding these corrupted witches. He couldn't get emotional about visiting the crime scene. A heavy sigh came from the compact. "I knew Rebecca Yarrow for a long time, Theo. Just... keep your head above the water, alright? She would haunt my ass from beyond the grave if I let you self-destruct working on her case."

"I'm going to do my job, Captain."

He snapped the compact shut to disconnect their call and stormed from the upturned mess his bedroom had become. Drawers had been ripped from the dresser, and clothes were strewn everywhere. The full-length mirror was shattered, the result of his now-bleeding fist flying through it. The room was a reflection of the tumbling emotions slamming themselves around in his brain, all trying to break free as tears or screams.

Theo had to shut it down. At least for now. He owed it to Rebecca to do his fucking job and find out who killed her.

The world around him finally came back into focus, and he realized his car was probably still parked at the SIA lot since Rebecca had given him a ride home. "Shit!" He couldn't think around the cacophony of emotions cluttering his head. Nothing could break through the chaotic howling of sadness and anger he was feeling right now.

Throwing the door open to storm out the condo, Theo's booted foot stepped on a small lump beneath the doormat laid in the hallway. Part of him was totally uninterested in investigating further, more focused on how the hell he was going to get to headquarters without running three miles, but the rational side won out and he flipped the edge of the mat to reveal what hid beneath.

The familiar teddy bear keychain attached to his car fob laid face up, its hand-stitched eyes staring up at the ceiling. Rebecca had sewn that keychain and given it to Theo on his second week as her partner. The fact it laid in front of his door now sent a fresh wave of sorrow washing through him. She had dropped off his car before she died, just like she said she would.

Slowly, painfully, Theo bent down to pluck the bear from the ground, cradling it in the palm of a shaking hand. His vision blurred from tears threatening to spill over as he stared at it.

"I'm coming to you, partner."

His pocket vibrated, warming to the touch as he pulled it out in a daze. Captain Tate had sent the coordinates mapped, the image wavering slightly on the smooth surface of the scrying mirror. Theo was unfamiliar with that area, but he knew enough to assume it was in the middle of the forest that surrounded the rebuilt town of Salem.

The overwhelming sense of despair burned away beneath the bomb of sheer, absolute fury that dropped into his chest and spread rapidly through his body. Theo's legs moved on their own as he rushed down to the basement garage beneath his condo building, the car's fob gripped tight in his hand to feel the intensifying vibrations that signaled his proximity to it. Theo turned the corner to the floor below at the fob's prompting and found his agency-issued black sedan sitting just on the other side.

The sight of it made Theo choke on the lump of emotions still burning and writhing in his chest, just beside his rapidly-beating heart.

Through the windshield, he could barely make out the white paper bag, distinct with its stamped logo of the twenty-four-hour diner they frequented. As Theo opened the door the handwritten note beneath the picture of a pig dressed in an apron became visible. It was Rebecca's handwriting in the black ink of her fountain pen.

Take it easy. We'll solve these cases together, partner.

"Yes, yes we fucking will," Theo swore to Rebecca, to the lunatics in that fucked-up coven, to whatever divine entity was listening. *We will stop these power-hungry assholes, if it's the last thing we do.*

Chapter Six

The car felt empty even as Theo sat inside, idling at the entrance of the hiking trail, without his mentor sitting beside him cracking some corny joke. She had become more than a coworker. Rebecca managed to lure out friendly conversation over coffee or late night dinners, offering helpful advice on more than just how to survive in the force. Simultaneously, she had honed his attention to detail and became his second set of eyes at a scene.

He couldn't bear to open the innocent white take-out bag she left in his car when Rebecca dropped it off, but from the smell he knew it was his favorite glazed donuts she knew he loved. The simple gesture, in light of all that's happened since he saw her last, was almost enough to throw him off the edge of sanity.

He knew he would have to start doing this alone, but this was not at all how he imagined it. Her retirement party was scheduled for next week, but now it turned into a wake. Her absence rattled Theo's confidence, maybe for the first time in his whole career. Plenty of partners had come and gone—some more unexpectedly than others—but none seemed to care about his personal well-being quite as much as Rebecca. She stood in as a mother figure, and her loss cut just as deeply as losing his real mother.

Still trapped in a cage of vengeful wrath, he threw open the car door and flung himself out, barely waiting for it to slam shut before storming off down the foot-worn path. The crime scene itself was buried deep in the thick woods, but once he stepped onto the trail he hardly needed directions.

The bitter, rancid stench of dark magic hit his delicate senses like walking by days-old roadkill. Automatically, his nose wrinkled, but he followed the path for a few yards as it wound around large boulders and towering redwoods. With every step, his stomach sloshed uneasily.

This is just another scene, treat it like any other case, he berated himself and shook out his shoulders.

Theo followed the horrid sensation as it deviated off the path and farther into the trees. After a long while of weaving through them, he stepped to the edge of a small glade not unlike the one from the first ritual. Man-made, hastily created with haphazardly-cut trees and fresh shavings nestled among the trampled grass and dead leaves. And in the center sat a red-stained altar, really a wide log cut longways and propped on four stumps. More black rope wound around the roughshod altar, and those are what Theo kept his eyes locked on as he stepped up to the barrier laid by the tracker squad who found the ritual site.

Blessedly, no one was here now to watch Theo's emotional breakdown.

The closest body part was a leg cut—more like brutally sawed—off and propped against a stump like a garden hoe set against a shed. The casual way it leaned against the stump was enough to make him gag on the sheer disrespect, and Theo's eyes hadn't even made it to the body. It was completely bare, no sign of clothes or a shoe in the area.

The way those fucking witches treat these people's bodies is mortifying. How does someone do this to another living person?

It was a monumental effort to drag his gaze from the grotesque leg and pull his attention back to the altar. Respect for the woman he knew warred with duty to find who the twisted motherfuckers were who decided their personal hunger for more power was worth more than a human life.

Her body was tied down across the chest and thighs, although he guessed there had been more restraints on the wrists, ankles and throat before the parts had been removed. The cleaved pieces had taken up strategic places around the clearing, similar to the leg in relation to where they had been on the body—the hands across from each other to his left and the legs to his right to create a square within the rough circle of the forest border. Rebecca's head, however, was placed in mock reverence at the top of the altar with the rest of her, sitting on her neck as if to see with lifeless eyes what had become of her body.

Theo finally stepped across the barrier as if it didn't exist, emotions flaring to a volcanic high as he stormed up to his partner. He tried to keep his last memory of her alive firmly in his mind. Theo didn't want to remember Rebecca butchered and sacrificed by some crazy bitches on a power trip.

All the other pieces of her body appeared to have been hacked apart with dull blades, maybe even torn off when it got too tiring to cut through bone and muscle, but there was a very deliberate incision across her lower abdomen. The organs were jostled all out of place as if ripped out and shoved back in. Theo's losing battle against the nausea finally tipped, and he staggered a few steps before bending over and violently retching.

Tears mixed with the snot and vomit as he stared down at the ground dazedly and tried to blink them away.

He couldn't do it. He couldn't look at her anymore.

But Theo could do something.

His hands shook violently as he reached inside his jacket for the small notebook he kept with him all the time. The familiarity of the smooth leather cover was his only comfort, opening it to the inside to trace the initials etched there. It was the only thing he kept from his dad, and now he wished more than ever for his help.

T.S.

Theo pulled the pen where it had been wedged between the spine and cover, taking precise notes of everything he saw since arriving at the ritual site. He knew there was nothing else he could do for Rebecca now, but there was someone else who could. A particular witch who could tell him exactly who did this. Someone he would kill with his own hands if it was the last thing he did.

Theo's hands slammed against the door, pinning the paper with his notes between his palm and the smooth wood. He knew Dorianne was standing on the other side; her presence was a cloying, heady aura that smothered him like a wet blanket. His fingers curled in anger and crumpled the already-ragged notepad paper.

What could I have done to save Rebecca? Who do I need to go after? Fuck that, who do I need to kill?

The square flashed its bright yellow, taking the sheet with it. A slight rustle told him she had caught the page before it fell to the floor. His breathing was too loud in his ears as he pressed his forehead to the door and squeezed his eyes shut, trying his best to hold himself together until he could make it home to fall apart. The silence was almost unbearable, quiet enough to leave Theo wallowing in the darkest thoughts, as she read over his notes.

"Theo..." Her voice was pitched low in what seemed to be sympathy. "I'm... sorry. Rebecca was... a kind soul."

He snapped back, fully ruled by his unchecked rage. "How the hell would you know? Did you even talk to her?"

"No. But she would talk to me."

That innocent admission struck a chord in Theo. The flames he had stoked in his chest were doused a little when he realized she knew Rebecca much longer than he did. Theo's forehead thumped against the door again, eyes closing to hold back the waves of sadness leading the next stage of grief. "Yeah... She did that a lot." In spite of himself, a pained chuckle escaped his mouth. "She should have been an interrogator. Rebecca had a way of getting to you in the best way possible."

A gravel-rough sound echoed from the other side of the door like it was ricocheting off vast walls, trying to escape the house. It took a moment for Theo to realize it was laughter. Laughter from someone who didn't use her voice often.

The revelation broke his heart just a little more. Maybe she didn't connect to Rebecca the way he did, but she did share many years of a working relationship. *That had to count for something, right?*

"This... these notes are similar to the last ritual you described."

"Yeah," Theo replied wearily. He turned to press his back against the door and slid down roughly to land on his ass. The pain of landing so hard against the porch didn't even register through all the grief. "Some kind of death runes were found around the first sacrifice and... and Rebecca's neck. They were around the throat of the witch you identified as well. Whoever controls them killed her, too."

"The hunger for more power is a terrible one. It eats those who crave it alive. I have lost... many sisters and brothers to it, both as sacrifices themselves and the ones who sacrifice others."

It took a moment for Theo to realize she was talking about her old coven. The pain woven through her voice resonated in his own chest, as if her loss was his. It was irrational, illogical, but the connection he felt with Dorianne was undeniable. "I'm sorry to hear you lost people too. It's... pretty shitty, what they're doing." He hesitated, wondering if he could push a little farther to learn more about Dorianne. "Which one did you belong to?"

A heavy silence fell between them. He couldn't tell if Dorianne was even there anymore, she was so still and quiet. That overwhelming sense of magic still hovered though. It expanded beyond the door he leaned against and wrapped around his shoulders like the heavy weight of a comforting blanket.

"The Black Staff."

She had been silent so long her answer had startled Theo, pushing away from the door in surprise. "What was that?"

It seemed like she was hesitant to repeat herself. "The coven, the only practitioners insane and twisted enough to use death runes like that, is called the Black Staff. Although, it wasn't that way when I was a member. They have been in Salem almost from the New Beginning. When the coven was created, the witches were devoted earth pact-bearers. But... a corrupted witch took over and, in turn, recruited other witches with similarly bent minds. They have been a scourge on this earth ever since."

The revelation was shocking, to say the least. Theo didn't think Dorianne had even kept up with what was going on outside her home, much less have any useful knowledge on the history of a coven. "Who runs the coven now?"

"I... am unsure."

Theo figured that was a little ambitious to hope she would know, as disconnected as she was from the world. "Well, hopefully you can give me some clues from those notes? I can... I'll head back to SIA and see what else I can find out in the meantime. I guess just send me a message when the drawing is ready."

Paper rustled from the other side of the door again. "Certainly. And, Theo?"

"Yeah?"

"Just... be careful. The frequency of these rituals are too close. I fear the coven will try something desperate soon. They are preparing for something. It's impossible to tell what kind of magic they are trying to weave, gathering this much ritualistic power, but it is definitely for malicious intent."

He stared at the wooden door as if hoping he could see through it. Or maybe that it would open so he could see Dorianne's face himself. Theo's instincts told him she was hiding what she really knew about this Black Staff coven. He wasn't sure enough to accuse her outright of lying, and he couldn't afford to piss her off right now by confronting Dorianne about it.

Did she care about my safety as a partner? Or... was she as interested in me as a person as I was in her?

She wouldn't tell him outright... but maybe he could find something in her house to help him learn more about the coven. Surely, she had some diaries or tomes she kept, as someone knowledgeable about the Black Staff and their witches.

"Right," he finally replied, realizing he had left Dorianne in silence for too long. With a groan he rose to his feet and brushed off the back of his jeans. "I'll be in touch. And, thank you, Dorianne."

He waited, hoping she would cave and give him another morsel of information with a hand resting against the door. Dorianne seemed to hesitate as well, something brushing on the other side of the door. Maybe she was leaning against the other side, or even pressing her hand against the same spot he did. Theo focused hard, trying to communicate without words how desperately he wanted to talk with her face-to-face.

I want to see you. I need to see you. Let me in, Dorianne.

"Wait..." Her voice was urgent, as if afraid he was going to walk away. Theo hadn't planned on it, hoping she would let him sit on her porch undisturbed. "Do you... want to talk about her? Rebecca? From those I've lost, I found it cathartic to... remember them. Fond memories, and the like."

Theo's chest cracked open just a little wider. Between those cracks the reluctant warmth of hope, the desire for companionship, leaked through. "I would... really like that. If you're not busy or anything."

Where did this timidity come from?

Something brushed against the door and slid down, like Dorianne had also sat on the floor to settle in. "I would be happy to sit with you, Theo."

At her gentle encouragement, the dam straining against the raging current of his grief broke loose. He talked about his first week at the agency, how he didn't really feel like he fit in with the talented agents that surrounded him, and Rebecca's bright smile when Theo walked into their shared office and clapped him warmly on the back like a long-lost friend.

Theo shared their first investigation. His first blunders. How Rebecca would patiently but firmly correct his mistakes. Everything. Once he let it go, the memories flowed out in a satisfying release. The tightness that threatened to crush his heart loosened the slightest bit with every hour he sat on Dorianne's porch. And she never once made the indication she was bored, or needed to leave, or had an opinion on much of anything.

Dorianne sat, and she listened. Even when Theo was done talking and the sun peeked over the horizon and brought with it vibrant pink-and-gold colors staining the sky, she sat on the other side of the door in comfortable silence. Every minute that passed in her soothing presence fed Theo's need to know more about her, more than Dorianne seemed willing to share from the safety of her house.

It was irrational and all-consuming at this point.

He was going to find a way inside. Dorianne couldn't hide in there forever. Theo wouldn't let anyone else hide the truth from him, not even her. As he wordlessly stood and made his way down the sidewalk to the car, the gears in his mind were already whirring and throwing steam, concocting a plan to break into the Mother of Shadow's house and finally quell his burning curiosity.

You're only meant to use this magic on the dead, Dorianne. This is irrational.

Shadows drifted around her feet, playing with the off-white lace hem on the full skirt as it brushed across the dull cement floor. The snapping tendrils gave away how uneasy they were at her so-called "erratic nonsensical behavior." Dorianne snorted at the advice. "Since when are *you* the voice of reason?"

Since you shoved yours off the cliff of insanity, it seems. I heard its screams all the way down until it shattered on the rocks of stupidity.

"Well, aren't you the poet when it comes to insulting my intellect."

They didn't take the easy bait. *What do you hope to accomplish, spying on that SIA rat? I can already tell you he's as bland as the one before him, and the one before her. Magicless, weak, useless—*

"Enough."

What? It's true. Weaklings are hardly worth the air they breathe.

"I'm sure whoever spat you out of hell says the same about you, weakling."

Her bitter disdain made the darkness roil and bubble like a frothing ocean, becoming substantial enough to displace the wooden table beside Dorianne and rattle glass bottles on nearby shelves as it sloshed up toward the ceiling. Wind whipped around the atelier, ruffling her skirts and pulling pieces of white hair from its simple braid. It was seething in rage.

You watch your tongue, witch, the sibilant voices spat and screeched. *I was once a feared legion of demons who walked beside Azazel himself as he took over this pitiful world! It was filled with pathetic, weak mortals who thought they knew what they wanted but no power to take it!*

"Uh-huh," she muttered, unfazed by its temper tantrum. "And how does it feel, being tied to and commanded by one of those, as you said, 'weak mortals?'" Dorianne used air quotes with one hand, the other holding a stack of ingredients she needed for spellcasting to set on the table by her easel.

The loathing practically billowed from her shadowy companion. *It is a bitter pill to swallow, to be sure. Especially when I have to sit by and watch you do something stupid such as this.*

"You really are no fun."

She picked up the first brush–the bristles made of her own hair as the spell required and fastened to an oak handle she carved–and began the meticulous process of painting the runes across the canvas in black. This part was always the most cathartic, something she had done so many times she could close her eyes and the hand's memory would take over writing. Starting in the very center and wrote in an outward spiral, the script creating its own kind of scrawling—but beautiful—art. Every symbol drew into it just a sliver of the abundant shadows now drifting idly around the room, small tendrils slipping in between the bristles to merge with the wet paint.

"That's that," Dorianne murmured after a half hour of bending over the canvas. "Now it's your turn."

The shadows grumbled, but in the end had no choice but to complete its end of the pact between them, now precisely drawn on the canvas as a reminder and a contract all at once. The hollowing draw of Dorianne's share of the magic pulled at something deep in her chest. The only remainder of earth magic she had been born with withered under the dark shroud of the bond shared with the horde. Really it was more of an uneasy truce between an unstoppable force and an indomitable will, a stalemate between Dorianne and the demons turned to shadow.

I hope you are prepared to accept the consequences of what answers you seek.

Ignoring the shadows yet again, Dorianne set her spelled brush aside for a wider, denser version to whitewash over the runes, creating a satisfyingly blank canvas for the real art to rest upon. The drawing room darkened noticeably, shadows creeping up the walls and looming over her shoulders, tendrils slithering to wrap themselves around Dorianne as she became absorbed in her painting. Obsessed with capturing every angle, every smooth plane, and every hair placed intentionally but disheveled across the forehead of a face she had only glimpsed through the peephole of her door.

Of Theo Slater.

Even though his face would not be the final product, Dorianne spent an exorbitant amount of time capturing every detail from memory and placing them carefully on the canvas. Meals were forgotten. Breaks, a forgone conclusion. Any kind of personal regard was completely thrown to the side to finish this portrait as quickly as she could possibly manage, while at the same time giving loving attention to each minute detail. She poured every longing she harbored in her shriveled little heart—meeting Theo in person, throwing open the door and stepping outside for the first time in two hundred years, damning the consequences of actions made by a young, naïve girl—into the careful strokes Dorianne painted onto the canvas.

Usually she used this spell in a quicker charcoal sketch, but the longer the art takes to complete, the clearer the details of the subject's death are depicted. With every brush stroke, the spell devoured more and more of her magic, doubly so, since the subject was still alive. Theo still had a lifetime to evade death, and that uncertainty had a toll. At this point, Dorianne wasn't using her shadows to see through the eyes of the dead to report how they died.

She was forcing the shadows through time itself to see into the future, to find how Theo will die by transforming the portrait she created to one portraying his last moments. And even worse, she was doing this for purely selfish reasons. Reasons she didn't want to confront or rationalize. Dorianne wanted to *save* him. She was driven by a fascination never felt before, a connection to a mortal who wouldn't live forever, but could possibly live longer with her intervention.

It wasn't love. It couldn't be. But perhaps... attraction. Admiration? Dorianne respected Theo's passion for his goals. Maybe even envied him the drive to move forward toward something. He spoke so highly of Rebecca even as he mourned her loss, sitting on the other side of Dorianne's door. Theo had a small circle of people he cared for, that much was obvious. Maybe Dorianne just imagined it, but she felt like he had taken her by the wrist today and pulled her into that circle, too.

Now, she found a motivation of her own. Dorianne would make sure Theo lived long enough to accomplish what he had dedicated his whole life for.

She owed him at least this much.

Hours of hunched posture and intense concentration later, a perfect replication of Theo's attentive stare looked out at her, brows drawn over eyes shaded gray but in life were a brilliant blue. Dorianne stepped back, slightly unsteady on her feet, to admire the strong cheekbones and sharp cut of his bearded jaw.

Her hand reached out for the silver dagger sitting on the table beside her. She sliced deeply into her opposite wrist and flung blood onto the pensive face to activate the second phase of the spell. Ruby droplets dribbled down the canvas, one in particular trickling down as if it came from his own left eye.

"Show me your death, Theo Slater."

Black miasma oozed from the portrait as if it too was bleeding paint. Beneath the bloody mixture the lines Dorianne painted so thoughtfully writhed and slithered into a new piece altogether. And it was not a face she could bear to look at.

For the first time in at least a century, frustrated tears burned her eyes.

Is now a bad time to say we told you so?

She didn't even respond to her tormenting shadows, turning from the canvas and sweeping from the drawing room, dread and self-loathing nipping at her heels as she fled. The shadows lingered, gently caressing a truth that Dorianne refused to face herself. She should have never let curiosity get the best of her. She should have just drawn what Theo asked for and sent him on his way. But she listened to that niggling doubt that these rituals were more than just a grab for more power. They were trying to lure her out using anyone who could be associated with her. The fact the Black Staff was going after SIA agents now was telling enough—they were getting desperate. And the SIA, specifically Theo, was getting too close to finding the reason for their rituals.

Soon, Dorianne would be forced to act. And she did not think they wanted to see how far *she* would go for one such as Theo Slater.

Chapter Seven

What am I doing here?

Of all the half-cocked plans Theo had come up with—of which there were only really a handful—this one had to be the least-thought through of them all. Whoever decided to just show up to a witch's house uninvited usually had a death wish. He was planning to *break into* a witch's house, and Theo didn't want to manifest what horrible outcome that would bring. The determination from this morning had now died to a barely-there sizzle, doused by the cold realization Dorianne could actually kill him if she wanted.

Swallowing the rising doubt, he set his hands firmly on the nondescript front door of Dorianne's home.

Immediately Theo's hands glowed a fearful, burning orange, the brightness growing in intensity as he gritted his teeth and willed the invisible wards to break. Really, he didn't have a particular plan on how exactly he would do that. When he would accidentally walk through the barriers set by SIA trackers around the crime scenes, he usually wasn't *thinking* about them. Theo would be so focused on everything else that he would just... walk through. Much to the dismay of the trackers. He hoped it was the intent that let him get through the barriers.

Otherwise, Theo would be shit out of luck and his plan would die an early death.

The pain was quickly approaching excruciating. It felt like he was pushing against the sturdy metal wall of a burning building. If his palms weren't completely charred after this, Theo would be shocked. The heat radiated up his wrists and to his elbows, filling his veins with molten agony. The invisible wall bowed, giving just the smallest amount. But it was enough to bolster Theo's strength and give another mental shove against the flaring spells. Now, he was pushing against the sun itself with how hot the barrier burned.

"Come on," he growled through a clenched jaw. "Open the fuck up!"

This wasn't right.

Dorianne didn't want him there.

She didn't need anyone.

Theo knew all that. He was breaking in for purely selfish reasons. He needed to know if Dorianne was connected to his parents' deaths, either directly or otherwise. Why did she used the same kind of dangerous runes? Was it because she was a part of the Black Staff coven? Did she hide because she was guilty, or because she was afraid of something?

He had to find the truth. This was what he had been working toward for over twenty years.

Suddenly, the wards gave with the deafening blast of a cannon, throwing his body clear off the porch like a child throwing a doll to sprawl halfway into the street. It was a small mercy his head managed to miss the front bumper of his car parked at the curb. However, it slammed back into the cold cobblestone of the road hard enough to leave him dazed and breathless.

But he did it. The oppressive weight looming around Dorianne's house had dissipated, a fog burning away with the light of day. There was nothing stopping him from getting inside now.

That was Theo's first naïve thought as he slowly recovered, groaning in pain as he pushed himself up onto his elbows and rolled his head on a sore neck. Then, common sense returned and Theo assumed Dorianne would know the protective wards were broken, and would be none too happy about it. His eyes crept slowly up the exterior of the brownstone to the third floor window.

He wasn't expecting to see her silhouette against the simple white drapes.

Oh, shit.

She was definitely pissed.

He was already in deep waters. At this point the only way out was through. He could only hope the leviathan lurking just beneath the water was more merciful than the rumors whispered around the supernatural community. No one at the SIA headquarters was gunning for his position as her keeper, to be sure.

"I'm coming to you, D," Theo muttered, mostly to hype his dwindling confidence.

She shifted as if she could hear him from her window. The drapes fluttered slightly, the dim violet light flickering out suddenly and hiding her in shadow.

He mounted the steps slowly, reaching out cautiously to grip the brass doorknob. Even slower, he rotated his wrist, the chilled surface of the metal its own special torture against his sensitive palm. Surprisingly, the latch gave with a soft snick, unlocked behind the powerful wards he broke.

Unless Dorianne had unlocked it herself.

Theo tried to ignore the feeling he was a bug wandering aimlessly into the spider's web. He needed answers. He needed to confront Dorianne and rip away the shroud of mystery she wrapped herself in so tightly. Mustering his last shreds of courage, Theo pushed open the deceptively heavy door and stepped over the threshold to enter the dark foyer of Dorianne's home.

Dorianne sank deep into the shadows in the corner of the large foyer, drawn to the incredible amount of magic gathering outside her front door and ready to pounce, the whirling vortex of a powerful dark spell held in her palm and pulsing with deep indigo light as she warred with the idea of whether or not to snuff his life for his crime. She watched Theo creep inside and carefully close the door behind him, a mix of shock and betrayal pulling the corners of her scarred lips down in a scowl. The darkness tittered excitedly at the prospect of fresh blood, a new victim to play with, to the point it strained against Dorianne's tight reins. Her teeth ground in irritation, a welcome distraction to the alluring whispers of the demons she was bound to.

How did he managed to break the wards?

"Fucking selfish child," she muttered too quietly for Theo to hear as he walked slowly across the thick burgundy carpet. "I should just let him get torn apart."

The shadows balked. That would end the fun much too quickly for their liking.

Tendrils crept along the floor from her corner, inky black as they nipped at his heels with malicious intent. He cursed colorfully and whipped around, looking all over with those honeyed hazel eyes wide open to see what could have pulled him off his feet.

Leave him be, she scolded internally to the dark presence she associated with the living shadows. *His stupidity probably gives a bad taste. You don't want to risk eating him.*

It would be a mercy to the world.

Their voice sounded like many and one at the same time, a chaotic choir of shrill sounds and baritone rumbles as they spoke directly into her mind. No one else Dorianne ever encountered were able to hear them. It was disconcerting to listen to, at the very least. In this way, however, they made for excellent spies and interesting companions in her self-imposed confinement.

Nice try. I know what you're trying to do.

They hissed, amused. *Just let us scare him a little.*

That's a thought, she mused.

Her shadows gurgled their unnatural laughter in her mind as she melted into their cover. With the purposeful lack of lighting in the house, traveling through the pools of darkness gathered along the walls was effortless. Even with his keen senses, Theo wouldn't be able to see her unless she wanted him to. The imagining of his horrified face as she materialized from the dark brought a wicked smile to her lips even as it twisted her stomach with unease.

What would *he think, if he ever saw me?*

"Hello?" he called down the dim hallway, sparsely decorated except for a black carpet runner and a gilded frame holding one of her original paintings. It depicted a darkened forest line under the bright light of a full moon, with the faintest impression of animals lurking between the trees with bright eyes that stared straight out from the canvas.

His wary gaze caught on the painting and a visible shiver shook his shoulders. "I should have known she was into creepy art like this."

Dorianne rolled her eyes in an unseen response, strolling right alongside him in the dark as he moved farther down the hallway. Due to her affliction, any light in the house was a dim purple flame-bulb flickering just bright enough to be useful. Her sight was perfect in total darkness, so they were hardly for her benefit. Dorianne only kept them around to keep up the farce someone normal lived in the house from the outside looking in, showing the lights turn on and off through the curtained windows.

"How big is this fucking house?"

He bumbled through the opened double doors into the formal dining room and promptly nailed his hip on the corner of the heavy table that took up the majority of the floor. A colorful and rather creative litany of curses spat from his mouth as he tried to right himself, knocking into the nearby chair in the dark instead. She chuckled silently in spite of herself at the impromptu comedy skit.

More hissed laughter tickled Dorianne's ear as they watched him stumble around the room in the dark.

How long do you think he will last?

Her eyes rolled. *He is a crime scene investigator for unregistered ceremonies. It would take more than your childish pranks to shake him, I'm sure. Just don't kill him if you can manage. I'm already on the SIA's black-list without hiding the body of their golden child.*

You're such a bore.

A chilling wind swirled through the room, ruffling Dorianne's pale hair before gaining strength and slamming against Theo's broad back. His palms slapped against the top of the polished dining table to avoid landing face-first against it. That prone position, him bent over that table panting heavily in shock, did something to Dorianne. Something... dark, and alluring shifted inside her, awakening in mild interest.

The urge to run her fingertips up his spine in that position had lifted her arm halfway, pulling her to his prone form just a few steps away before she stopped herself. Dorianne couldn't be here, not now. Not with something so enticing as Theo tiptoeing around the edges of her restraint, teasing her to let go just for a moment and indulge in the prey that had willingly forced himself into her refuge.

"Are you fucking with me right now, Dorianne?" he called to the room, shoving himself up and whirling around to look for a threat, someone to retaliate against.

He had no idea the things she imagined doing to him right now. Seeing him in person now—all lean muscle on a tall frame, dark hair and golden hazel eyes as he prowled around her dark home—shifted some of those fantasies to more... savory experiences. He was not nearly that attractive through the peephole of her door.

"Come on. I just want to talk. I just want to see you... actually see who listened to me while I bled my fucking heart out on your porch."

No, he doesn't. I can't let him in.

It was the tinge of desperation in his voice, though, that gave her pause. It stirred that slumbering beast in her again, poking at it incessantly to awaken that feeling of being wanted by someone. Dorianne didn't think it was even possible for someone to be interested in her for more than her power. Her own sister literally ate her alive for it.

The shadows knew what was best. *"Theo..."* they called faintly, their voice now a perfect mimicry of her own. *"Come find me, Theo."* The tantalizing come-hither lilt of her mimicked voice bothered Dorianne. Surely, he wouldn't fall for such a cheap trick.

"Damn it, D, can you tone down the creep factor? We can sit and talk like adults, right?" Theo swallowed it bait and hook like the unsuspected trout he was, following the shadows' call back through the hall to the main foyer. They had thrown the voice so that it sounded like Dorianne had called from the top of the sweeping staircase to the second floor.

I cannot believe he fell for that. You made me sound like a prostitute.

Men have a one-track mind, the shadows were particularly smug. *This will be fun.*

If you say so.

She allowed herself to be swallowed whole by the darkness and swept up the wall to skirt the crown molding along the ceiling, floating in the air like a wraith and trailing after Theo and his profound stupidity.

Theo swore the staircase was putting on a show, stairs creaking ominously as if they threatened to break despite their clean, maintained appearance. The awful dim lighting alone was enough of a threat to send him tumbling down to the bottom with how it distorted his depth perception, but on top of that skittering of crawling things in every dark corner set him on high alert.

"This is bullshit, Dorianne!" he called out to nothing, gripping the handrail with whitened knuckles. "You know I'm not going to do anything to you! We're on the same team! I just need your help with a cold case and got tired of talking to a damn door! This could possibly help us find who killed Rebecca!"

He wasn't sure if she could sense his true motivation—to investigate why she used the same death runes found at the murder of his parents—but he didn't think she would respond well to a straightforward interrogation. He needed to appear as if he was on the back foot, at a disadvantage, to hopefully lure her into giving him the information he had been hunting the last twenty years.

Unfortunately, his plan was working too well. Theo indeed felt like he was on the back foot, about to plummet to his death on this ridiculously noisy staircase.

More paintings lined the wall in regular intervals along the curving staircase, a progressive set of landscapes focused on a cemetery through the seasons. As Theo passed each piece, the paintings shuddered on their frame wires and hissed, as if ghosts from the graves themselves were trying to escape.

Theo glared at the closest one. It was a deceptively cheerful one with sprouting flowers and the hints of spring scattered among the tombstones. "A bit over the top, D. Not that I don't believe this place is ridiculously haunted, because I'm very sure it is. You've made your point! I'm adequately creeped out, so can we sit and talk like adults now? Maybe over tea?"

A dark, claw-tipped hand shot out from the spring-themed art, nearly catching Theo across the face as it swiped at him. He flinched hard enough to throw himself off-balance on the unforgiving wooden stairs, rocking back on his heels with arms pinwheeling and expletives spewing from his mouth as if that would help pull him back up. Just as his center of gravity shifted against him the beastly hand caught hold of a flailing wrist and flung Theo forward up the stairs. The tall bridge of his nose slammed against the edge of a step, a sickening crunch the telltale sign of the cartilage breaking. A pain-drenched groan slipped from between his clenched teeth as blood gushed from his broken nose and pooled beneath his face on the dark wood.

It took Theo an excruciating amount of time to regain his composure and swat the stars circling his head away. One hand crept up to cover the sensitive skin that had split open on impact, literally adding insult to injury.

"What the actual supernatural fuck, Dorianne! Get the fuck out here or I'll haul you in to the SIA for assaulting your handler!"

Within the span of a racing heartbeat, the air grew impossibly heavy and ominously thick, an unseen threat looming like a guillotine blade about to drop on his neck. His breath sawed in and out through a jaw clenched as he tried to manage the pain of a smashed face and encroaching fear, the visceral kind of which he could not remember facing in his lifetime. The air misted as soon as it left his lips from how much the air had chilled.

If he didn't get the hint he was unwelcome, it was painfully obvious now with every throb of his face. "At this rate, I almost wish you would have let me fall," he snarked, hissing in pain as he gingerly touched the bridge of his nose.

Shadows coalesced on the top step, a shapeless mass swirling in an unnatural tornado until it twisted in on itself and morphed into the unsettling replica of a female body. Her face was not a face at all, just a blank space where facial features should be. A sharp chill shot down Theo's spine as its head bent down to look at him with an eyeless gaze. Even without a face, he felt a smugness radiating from it.

"What are you, some kind of familiar? I didn't think pact-bearers could have those," Theo mused with a comically altered voice from beneath the pinched bridge of his nose. "Look, I really don't mean D any harm. Do what you need to do to clear me of any kind of offensive magic you think I have. I'm a dud, I promise."

"Breaking through someone's wards would not really qualify you as a dud, would it?" The shadow's edges twitched and writhed in obvious anger as if it struggled to maintain its form, tendrils whipping out and snapping at the air. Faint shapes of beastly heads and monstrous claws flickered at the edges of the otherwise humanoid shape as if stretching it from the inside. It was unlike anything Theo had seen before, even from the training academy for the SIA.

"Again, what the hell are you? How can you act so independently?" Theo's curiosity obviously trumped his sense of self-preservation.

It hissed another mocking laugh. "Bold of you to assume I act on my own. Have you considered Dorianne is offended at your intrusion? Maybe she wants you dead, human."

"If she wanted me dead, I would not have made it past the front door."

"Or you could just be a cockroach who refuses to die." The dark shape drifted closer, ghostly legs reaching to the ground but dissipating in a cloud of unnatural black smoke that trailed behind it like the train of a dress. "Only moments ago you seemed to think she was trying to kill you. Make up your mind, roach. Are you dying tonight or not?"

Theo's eyes narrowed in a glare. "Preferably not, if I can help it."

"Then leave, *now,*" the shadow roared suddenly, frigid air blasting from it and an unseen force rattling the frames on the wall. Both almost sent Theo toppling backward again. "You are not wanted or needed here!"

"What are you hiding from, Dorianne?" he called out, trying to yell over the now-howling wind whipping around him. "Who is looking for you? The Black Staff coven?"

As suddenly as it started, the wind stilled, leaving behind that frigid, eerie silence again. Pressure built on Theo's body intense enough to make his ears pop, pushing in from all angles as if he were dragged to the bottom of a dark, deep ocean. He could barely even breathe, especially through a nose clogged with drying blood. Theo's guess must have been spot on.

"Tell me," he struggled to plead through the air thickened by magic. "I can help if you just *let me*!"

That pressure grew even stronger, becoming a massive hand that wrapped around his torso. Theo could feel his ribs squeeze inward and true fear crept up his throat. Something moved in the corner of his eye, possibly someone moving in the hallway and hid from his line of sight. He couldn't even turn his head to confirm or call out to Dorianne. Theo was firmly in the shadow's grasp.

The shadowy figure was in motion again. "You are very dense," it spat, floating farther away. Theo remained frozen in place but vibrated with a desperate need to follow it, knowing it would lead him to Dorianne. "If you're asking if an incredibly dangerous and spiteful coven of the darkest witches known to man are hunting Dorianne, wouldn't that be reason enough to keep the world at arm's length?"

As the entity drifted away, the hold on Theo's body loosened bit by bit. As soon as his legs were freed enough to move, he stumbled forward and barely caught himself from being further mutilated by the staircase with both hands gripping the railing. With a cautious eye on the hallway entrance, he crept up the remaining stairs and carefully pulled himself up to full height on the landing. His heart pounded so violently in its bone cage he thought he would have to chase it across the floor when it decided to burst straight from his chest.

It was obvious he was supposed to see his way out at this point. But Theo had come too far to give up his wild plan now. Whatever her shadow familiar threw at him would be worth the chance to meet Dorianne in person. Maybe even touch her...

"Why are you like this?" he muttered angrily to himself, even as he cautiously followed after the vicious guardian. "Fucking idiot, breaking into a witch's house, can't let it go..." Theo's personalized berating lodged in his throat when the shadow separated from the rest of the darkness and passed through a doorway dimly marked with a wall sconce.

But when his foot hit the burgundy carpeting of the hall, all hell literally broke loose.

In front of his very eyes a roiling mass of shadows culminated at the end of the short hallway, curling and crashing from wall to wall as if a dark ocean had been let loose to flush out anything with the misfortune to cross its path. Waves of teeth, protruding spikes, and liquid a suspicious viscosity similar to blood barreled toward him too quickly to dodge and swept Theo off his feet with incredible speed. A pained yelp barked from Theo's lips as his back was slammed up against the banister rail, the only thing keeping him from falling head-first toward the unforgiving wooden floor below.

Another spectral wave slammed him square in the chest, and another. Every impact knocked the breath from his lungs and wouldn't relent long enough for him to recover it. He reached behind to brace against the wooden railing in an attempt to collect his footing with no luck.

CRACK!

The last brutal hit broke something—or multiple things, like perhaps bones—across Theo's clavicle and rib cage as well as the sturdy banister against the small of his back. All two-hundred pounds of his mass was launched straight off the second floor landing, the fall impossibly slow as he watched the gnashing dark mass follow him over the edge. Theo's eyes widened to bulging as he realized his fate.

I'm going to die.

If the fall wasn't going to kill him, it would definitely debilitate him enough for this violent shadow assemblage to crush him to a bloody pulp. As he belatedly reached up his right arm to grasp onto nothing, Theo's back slammed against the unforgiving floor, the back of his head hitting in the next millisecond. He already knew something vital had broken in his spine from the splintering pain on impact, but the blow to his head pitched him straight into unconsciousness.

Theo's head lulled to the side. From beneath it, a vibrant pool of red blood gathered, creeping along the hardwood and filling in the grooves between the floorboards. From the broken banister, Dorianne looked on as the demonic shadows completely enveloped his lifeless body and pulled it with them back into the darkness.

Chapter Eight

The first sense to come back to Theo was smell. The antiseptic bite in the air was his first indication he was not in Dorianne's home anymore. The deep breath he tried to take in was quickly followed by a stabbing pain all along his ribs and chest, as if the bones were shifting uncomfortably. The bright fluorescent light offended his eyes when he tried to open them and he groaned loudly as the rest of his body caught up with what he already knew.

I'm in the hospital. Shit.

"Welcome back, Slater."

Slowly, gently, Theo turned his head on the crinkling sterile pillow cover to find his captain planted in a chair by the bed, his arms crossed across his broad chest and a stormy, dark look on his craggy face. Even a grown man like Theo cowered just a little at the imposing man.

"I'd like to ask what the hell you were doing to get dropped—literally—in this hospital bed, but I doubt I would like the answer. I'm sure you can imagine the chaos that ensued when the nurses went to roll a patient in here and found your busted ass instead."

"Wha... d'you mnn?" Theo's tongue felt heavy and sluggish, making coherent words difficult to create. Even keeping his eyes open long enough to hold a conversation felt daunting. The drugs being pumped into him via the I.V. piercing his right hand probably had something to do with his debilitated condition. Judging from how groggy he was, Theo was sure life without the numbing medicine would be close to unbearable.

The captain seemed able to discern his question. A heavy sigh blew from beneath his wiry copper beard and he lifted a hand to rub tiredly at his eyes. "You were... in bad shape. Most of your ribs are cracked, as well as a broken clavicle and fractured right hip. Your spine also has several fractures and herniated disks. The doctors assumed you were a suicide attempt until I got here to verify your credentials. You literally just appeared in an empty hospital bed."

It was a monumental effort for Theo to root around in his memories and scrape together the pieces of how he ended up here. Eyes drifting out of focus, he gazed beyond the captain to the blank white wall as he stumbled through the brain fog.

There was... darkness. And... claws. And the feel of my nose being smashed against something, a floor maybe?

"I... don't..."

Captain sighed again. "Whatever you got into, you have a guardian angel to thank for getting you here in time. You barely made it to avoid paralysis from the amount of damage to your spine, and had to be rushed into surgery to save what they could of your mobility."

A very real and unfathomable fear set in. "Am I... able t' walk?"

"The odds are good, but you have a long road of recovery."

Theo's strings had been cut, hopelessness leaving him slack and boneless on the sterile white bed. If he couldn't walk, he couldn't chase the people who killed his parents or Rebecca on his own. He would have to rely on a chair, or his new partner, or whoever would take time out of their lives to stop and help him. Theo fought for so long to be able to stand proudly on his own, only to be knocked down again.

No. This wasn't the end. It couldn't be. Even this can't stop me.

"When can I get out?" Determination burned away the grogginess, leaving Theo alert and stewing in impotent rage.

"The doctors want to keep you for a couple of weeks at least. Run some tests to see if there's lingering spells at work, set you up for therapy to regain motor—"

"So I'll be back on duty in a month." His tone left no room for debate. Unfortunately, the captain had enough bulk to make room for himself. Captain's brow lowered angrily and he huffed out through his nose.

"You'll come back when I damn well think you can. I'm placing you on administrative leave like I should have done when Rebecca died. And don't you think you can talk your way out of it this time," he ranted and effectively cut Theo off from doing exactly that. "Your caseload has been transferred to the tracker unit anyway. The witch consultant has gone missing."

Silence fell heavy over the room and Theo finally noticed the captain's fidgeting for what it was—unease. He was sitting here in a room with a comatose man while one of the most dangerous witches known to SIA was running rampant somewhere out of his reach.

A witch Theo should have been monitoring. A witch Theo most likely scared off when he broke into her house and ended up in a hospital for it, rightfully so in his opinion.

"How... wha-when?" He couldn't settle on which question to ask first. He needed to know everything.

"The day after I found you in this hospital, the trackers reported a massive spike in magic usage at her last known location. By the time they got there, an illusion had been laid and her house was gone."

Theo's heart rate rose, the monitor beside him tracking his growing anxiety. "Gone as in destroyed?"

Captain snorted. "If only. No, gone as in no longer there. The illusion was a perfect copy of her house, down to a functioning door and realistic interior. But when the trackers went to cast a locator spell, some kind of trap was sprung and they were knocked out for a few hours. They woke up to an empty lot with a sale sign out front and all the neighbors' memories wiped clean. Impressive magic, for sure."

Impressive, and terrifying. Something in Theo's aching chest writhed in trepidation, the captain's recounting of just how powerful Dorianne unsettled him like nothing before. He had stood on the other side of a door from her, or sat on her porch talking about nothing in particular, and not once felt like she was dangerous. But now...

Theo could have very well been the one who broke the seal between Dorianne and the outside world she hid from. She could be alone in that world being hunted down right now, all because of his stupid stunt.

I have to find her, Theo's conviction roared in his head. *I have to make sure she's okay.*

"Well..." The captain slapped his hands against his black-clad thighs. He was in his uniform still, so he must have come straight from headquarters to Theo's bedside and hadn't left to change. "My wife has been nagging me on the compact every other hour, so I probably need to report home before she unleashes her wrath. Can you manage to stay out of trouble until tomorrow morning?"

Theo smiled ruefully, despite the whirring gears in his head. "I'll try my best, Captain. Thank you for sitting with me."

"Your father would find a way to sucker punch me from the grave if he didn't think I was keeping an eye on you." The captain chuckled.

"You knew Dad?"

Judging from the obvious wince on his face, Theo figured he hadn't meant to drop that little morsel of information. "It was a long time ago, before he even met your mom. But yeah, Thomas and I went way back. And you're just like him, that stubborn bastard."

Before Theo could pin him down with more questions, the captain swept from the room and sidestepped the nurses who came to fill his place at Theo's bedside.

"How are we doing this evening, hon?"

Theo was too caught up in his thoughts to give more than an absent answer, leaving her to flit about the room, check his vitals and administer what he hoped was more pain medication. The dull aches of his battered body were beginning to make themselves known. And he could easily slip under the comfortable blanket of a drug-induced haze without worrying about the outside world, and issues he was in no shape to deal with in his current state.

Question after question pelted his conscience until he drifted into a healing sleep.

They sat around the round table—Mom, Dad and Theo. Mom made his favorite dinner, spaghetti with her homemade meatballs. She said it reminded her of her mom, who he never knew. Something happened to her, but Mom would never talk about it. But she always met with Theo's Grandma Barough—her grandma— once a month to "recharge," whatever that meant. Whenever he tried to ask, Mom always said, "I'll tell you when you're older."

Theo hated that excuse.

"Are you heading over to your grandma's tomorrow, love?" Dad asked between bites of green beans. "I was thinking of taking Theo to the park."

Theo bounced excitedly in his cushioned chair. "Can we go swimming in the lake? Can we? Please, please!"

Mom chuckled and brushed an errant piece of Theo's hair from hanging in front of his eyes. "I'll be gone for the night. There's been some... issues that have popped up that we need to take care of."

Theo's parents shared a look across the table, some emotion he didn't like being shared between them. Dad almost seemed... nervous. Or maybe worried? Did he think Mom wouldn't let them out past Theo's bedtime?

"Alright..." Dad finally answered, obviously biting something back. "Just keep me posted if, you know, you need me to pick something up."

"Thank you, hon."

The lovey-dovey eyes they shared made Theo want to gag.

"Dad, what time— " A pounding at the door, urgent and alarming, interrupted Theo's question. The sound startled him and made Theo drop the fork loaded with saucy noodles straight into his lap. He looked between Mom and Dad, wondering if they were expecting someone else to come for dinner.

They shared another concerned look. "I'll get it." Dad laid his napkin to the side and cautiously rose from his seat, the heavy chair squealing across the laminate flooring. "Why don't you go get Theo changed, love?"

"Dad," Theo whined. "I'm nine! I can change myself!"

Mom seemed to agree with Dad, though. "Come on," she urged. "I think your pajamas are in the laundry basket in our room, can you come help me fold the clothes?"

"But what about dinner?"

"Theo." Dad's voice sounded weird. It trembled slightly, like he was scared and angry at the same time. His hands were clenched at his side and he jumped when the pounding started up again at the door, this time so hard Theo swore he could hear the door crack under the blows.

"Come on, baby!" Mom's voice was high-pitched and an unnatural smile strained her lips. "Let your father help whoever is at the door. It sounds like someone may have an emergency."

Dad was in law enforcement. In Theo's child-like mind, it didn't seem strange someone would bang on their door for help. That's just what he did. He helped people. He didn't talk much about work, but sometimes his partner Mr. Tate would come over to visit. They would hole themselves up in Dad's office for hours, and Mom would make lots of coffee and snacks for them to eat. One time, Theo snuck to the door and pushed his ear against it as hard as he could. The door had heated up weirdly, like someone started a fire on the other side, but eventually he strained hard enough to hear part of a conversation they had been having.

They were talking about witches. And some kind of runes that were bad. And lots of people dying.

Theo never tried to listen through the door again.

Theo came along reluctantly as Mom wrapped her hand around his upper arm. Her grip was tight, almost too tight, as she pulled him around the railing and urged him up the stairs in front of her. Dad caught her eyes one more time and in that brief look said something Theo couldn't understand. Mom sniffled quietly and hurried Theo even faster to the second floor landing.

"Mom? What's going on?" He tried not to sound whiny and scared. Still, she shushed him gently and pushed a little harder on his back to walk faster.

They moved down the hall to the end and through the door to Theo's parents' room. A room he was very familiar with. A room that represented safety, a place he went to escape the nightmares that woke him in the night or he ran to after a bad day at school. Mom always had lavender and sage incense burning that was a balm to anything that bothered Theo.

"Baby," she turned him to face her fully and crouched to meet his eyes, "I'm going to close this door, and I need you to make sure it stays shut no matter what. No matter what you hear or what you see, do not let this door open until I come to get you. Do you understand?"

A note of desperation colored her voice, her eyes glassy with tears. But beyond that was a wrinkled brow and mouth set in determination. Something was going on that she wouldn't—or couldn't—tell Theo. But he wanted to be helpful. Theo didn't want to see his mom crying.

"Okay," he answered meekly.

She pulled him in tight, burying her nose in his messy brown hair and pulling in a deep breath, like she was trying to hold something of him inside her chest. Mom's fingers curled into the back of his sweater before letting go and pushing him toward the closet.

"Sit in here like you're playing hide-and-seek. Your dad or I will come find you, okay? Just don't open the bedroom door."

Theo nodded without understanding what was going on, but allowed himself to be pushed into the walk-in closet his parents shared and sank into a criss-cross position on the carpeted floor. "I love you, Mom."

Theo didn't know why it was so important to tell her that right now. Mom knew he loved her.

But Mom's lips twitched into that non-smile again. "I love you too, baby. So, so much."

With one more long kiss to the top of his head, Mom pulled herself away and left Theo sitting on the floor of the dark closet. A lone tear trickled down her cheek from the crack in the door he could see through before she closed the door between them completely.

The quiet snick of the bedroom door as it was locked felt final, like a fatal gunshot to the heart.

Theo curled into the smallest ball he could contort himself into, and there he hid for what felt like years until he mustered the courage to creep back down the stairs.

Theo awoke on a choked gasp, arms and legs flailing as much as he could bound up in bandages in the hospital bed. The poor nurse standing beside him became his lifesaver as Theo latched onto her arm with his right hand and continued to cough violently. It felt as if Theo had actually drowned in the nightmare and was struggling hopelessly to resurface from sleep.

"Shh, shh," the nurse cooed, patting his hand gently with her own. "You're fine. You're okay. Just relax."

He let her soothing voice lull him back to a less chaotic frame of mind, breathing still heavy but more controlled than the frantic panting he woke up with. "S-sorry," Theo finally stuttered out. "I... I haven't had th-that dream for a wh-while."

She smiled down at him with a look of patient understanding. Her badge identified her as S. Romero. "It's fine, hon. Sometimes the meds do funny things to your head. Seems like a bad nightmare for you to wake up in such a fright."

"Yeah..." He didn't want to elaborate more than that. This wasn't just a nightmare. "Can I have some water please?"

Nurse Romero's warm brown eyes—shot through with the jagged black lines typical of a magic user—showed nothing but concern and sympathy as she filled a paper cup from a pitcher by his bed. Her steady hand clasped both of his as they reached out to carefully take the water from her and Theo tried his best to not guzzle it all at once.

Without warning, her head jerked up as if someone yelled for her. Brow furrowed, she let out a heavy sigh and pat Theo on the head as if to console herself as much as him. The gesture reminded Theo of dusty old memories of his own mother doing the same.

"Apologies in advance for the noise. It seems like tonight is going to be particularly busy."

Theo was confused. "How do you know—"

A harried group of scrub-clad nurses bustled past the door left open to his room, chattering amongst themselves and snatching charts from the nurse's station. Very faintly, Theo's ears picked up incessant beeping and urgent alarms of several medical monitors farther down the hall.

"That's my cue," she explained, setting his chart back in its folder holder hanging on the wall by his door. "Lunch will be coming around shortly. I believe it's chicken noodle soup. Just call if you need me."

Nurse Romero left a baffled Theo prone in his bed, wondering what it was that had caught her attention before the machines went off. The pesky habit that honed his detective skills so finely wouldn't let this mystery rest. Unfortunately, all he had was vacant time to chew on the questions roiling around in his unsettled brain.

Chapter Nine

The SIA headquarters was teeming with gossip the day Theo was able to limp his way through the door almost four weeks later. Captain had set a patrol on his house the first week of physical therapy, which Theo thought was ridiculous and a waste of resources. All he did was call in to the office to see if there were updates on Rebecca's death. Apparently, that was enough of a trigger to prompt twenty-four hour monitoring to keep Theo out of duty until his appointed day back... officially tomorrow, but Theo dared anyone to keep him on his ass for one more day.

Rebecca's desk was pointedly empty. Her meticulously organized pens and files—the only thing organized about her, really—had been cleared away like she was never there. It was rubbed in his face that her killer was still running free as he sat heavily in his own chair across from hers. And now he probably fucked up any chance to find said killer by stupidly pissing off the only witch he knew that could literally put the information in his lap. The amount of self-loathing that sloshed around inside his brain smothered any fiery motivation he could muster up right now.

Theo hadn't realized how hard he was staring at the bare desk until a light touch to his right shoulder startled him. That was a novel experience. Usually, Theo was hyper-aware of his surroundings.

"Sorry to hear about Rebecca," a tracker—Theo identified from the green uniform she wore—gave her condolences in an emotion-filled voice. "We crossed paths often enough to know she was good people."

It took Theo a moment to recognize where he'd seen her before. She was one of the trackers at his first crime scene with Rebecca. Her name escaped his memory, so engrossed he was in taking everything in at the unsanctioned ritual site. That seemed like so long ago, even when it was just over a month. Enough time had passed for the chill to let up and trees to show green-tipped branches of new growth.

"Thanks," he replied blandly, trying to find a polite way out from under her hand. "How have the cases been going?"

Her face scrunched in frustration. "Pretty slow right now. I didn't realize how much we relied on the consultant until..." She trailed off, probably at the realization Theo was also attached to said consultant and her disappearance. He kept his eyes glued to the enchanted mirror as he waved his hand across it to access the database and prompted open the message window. "Sorry. Probably a sore subject, huh?"

He didn't deem that question necessary to answer. Maybe she could read the room and terminate this painfully awkward conversation she started. Unfortunately, Theo's inbox was very sad and empty, mainly focused on leftovers from a weekend party in the break room for whoever was hungry. Probably another of the captain's attempts to keep him out of the field as long as possible.

His next goal was finding anything posted on the cases he had been working on prior to landing himself in the hospital. But he couldn't snoop around the files with Agent Lewis—he finally remembered her name—breathing down his neck. Theo suspected she wasn't her by her own volition. This reeked of the captain's meddlesome prying.

"I need to get some more coffee," he lied through his teeth, gesturing to the lidded tumbler sat by his screen. She didn't need to know it was full. "Please keep me posted on the investigations."

He shoved away from the desk and nearly ran over Lewis's foot. His muttered apology was carelessly thrown over his shoulder as he snatched up his alibi and stalked off toward the break room. Thirty minutes into his first day back and Theo already needed a break from people. Not his best record.

"Slater!" Captain's roar from his office—two doors down and across the hall from his own—pushed Theo's shoulders to his ears. His hopes of avoiding confrontation today crumbled before his eyes.

"Shit."

Theo tried to hide his immense discomfort as he stepped into the captain's office. That same glowering expression greeted him from the other side of the captain's massive desk, built to take up the massive space of the office and the massive man who inhabited it. He couldn't imagine anyone else sitting in Killian Tate's chair and filling it the way he did, full of authority and austereness as he was. His hands rested casually on the desk with fingers intertwined over whatever paperwork he had been working on. Theo wasn't fooled.

The captain was ready to pounce. And Theo was the unfortunate prey that had caught his unblinking sky-blue gaze.

"What the actual ass-burning hell are you doing here, Slater? You're not due to be back in the office until tomorrow. Did you think you could just sneak around here under my nose?"

"I wasn't sneaking, per se," Theo grumbled. Already he felt like a scolded child who had snuck out of the house. Or in his case, snuck in.

Captain kept up the silent, fuming persona for a few more moments—just long enough to make Theo want to squirm—before he finally relaxed and pushed back from his desk, reaching his hands high up before lacing his fingers again and resting them on top of the bristle of red hair.

"You're gonna make me gray before I'm sixty, you know that right? You just cannot stand staying out of trouble, can you?"

"I feel like you're setting me up for failure. This line of work isn't exactly risk-free."

He dragged both hands down to scrub his face several times in frustration. "I cannot even—" Captain dropped his hands into his lap and heaved a heavy sigh. "Can we at least manage to stay out of the hospital, then."

Theo hesitated, not sure if he should ask the question burning in his throat. "What about... the consultant?" It hurt to even think of her name, much less say it.

"Don't even get involved in that shitshow." The captain's eyes sparked in annoyance. "That is solidly out of your jurisdiction as of now."

"Am I being disciplined?" As soon as the words left his mouth, Theo realized his incriminating mistake. He had been dropped in a hospital, not found at Dorianne's home when the tracking team went to investigate the power surge they caught. He hadn't told anyone about breaking in. His foggy memory had protected him when the captain was at his bedside, but now that he'd made a full recovery all bets were off. Tate could easily throw him into an interrogation room if he though Theo had any insight as to what happened that night.

Captain realized something had slipped. His eyes sharpened and in that moment, Theo understood why he was such a celebrated detective in his day. Nothing got by his notice. "As of now, no. Is there something I should be aware of?"

Theo inwardly kicked himself. He wasn't exactly good at lying. Beads of sweat formed at the nape of his neck and trickle uncomfortably down his spine, and his hand became slick as he moved to cross his arms across his chest in an effort to remain casual. A giant ball of nerves lodged in his throat that he tried to swallow without being obviously unnerved. If he couldn't talk, at least he couldn't lie.

After a few uncomfortable moments being scrutinized by the captain, Theo cleared his throat and rocked back a step. "Well, I'm going to grab some coffee and get paperwork done. Don't think I can get into trouble with that."

"Hmmm..." the captain muttered a non-answer, still watching Theo closely as he made his escape from the Captain's den. The moment Theo turned his back he feared claws in his back from a damning accusation. He thought he had escaped unscathed, when the captain's voice boomed behind him once more. One foot had already stepped over the threshold. *So close.*

"Theo," Captain spoke to his back. "Just... take care of yourself. For obvious reasons, I can't treat you like a son, but... your dad was a good man. I'd hate to see his legacy end with you."

Frustration burned in Theo's chest. He wanted to ask the captain just how close he was to Dad. The urge warred with his very limited sense of self-preservation to keep his secrets to himself. Any longer in the captain's office risked him spilling his guts.

Lips pressed tight, Theo turned his head to nod in his direction. He tried to avoid meeting his eyes. "Thanks, Captain."

Then he hurried off, already committed to what he needed to do. He had to find Dorianne. He had to make sure she was safe. Which meant he had to figure out how to use tracker magic yesterday, without the captain or any of his rats finding out. He couldn't rely on the trackers themselves, and looking anything up on the SIA systems would basically scream, "I'm looking up shit I shouldn't be, please ban me from entering the building."

Theo's only option was the old-fashioned way—by picking through the tomes collected from exterminated practitioners and stored in the headquarters' library. He didn't have to report *which* books he looked through. He only had to sign in and out. On a physical log. There was too much concentrated magic there to rely on the magic-driven computer system the rest of the organization used. The librarians couldn't even cast a simple spell to go find a book without the risk of setting off a tome's dormant defensive curse.

Committed to his new plan, Theo tried to keep his face blank and strode slowly as he created his alibi, biding his time until he could slip into the library unnoticed.

If Killian decided to yank Theo off the streets and miraculously let him stay in the SIA, he would definitely push to be condoned to the agency's library. For most agents, it would probably be the least desirable place to work, unable to use any kind of magic either for convenience or necessity. Everything in the cavernous hall was manual, down to the documenting of inventory and looking through the card catalog to find the tome that potentially held what he was looking for.

With the first step inside the dim two-story hall the energy felt different, a tension heavy enough to make Theo's skin pebble as the heavy door fell shut behind him. A long desk sat squarely in the middle of the central aisle with a thick binder sitting on top, open to the next blank line to fill in a name, date, and times of check-in and check-out. His hasty glance over the log showed the last name reported leaving over an hour ago.

Perfect.

Theo bypassed the visitor log, skirting the desk to wander farther into the SIA library. His right side, right over the stab wound that healed over to a gnarly scar, tingled like something skittered just under his skin. It was hard to tell if it was a reaction to the residual magic that clung to the books, or if it was all in his mind, a trauma reaction to the last time he set foot in headquarters and ended up bleeding out in front of Rebecca. His consciousness cringed from that memory immediately. Her death was too fresh, too raw for him to cope with rationally.

The agony drove him farther into the stacks, looking for the cabinet that held the archaic card catalog system the librarians had to use to document the tome intake and give some kind of order to the neatly-presented, but overwhelming, amount of shelves lining the hall. It was that moment—staring at what had to be at least a hundred little drawers that pulled out at least two feet a piece—that a moment of clarity hit Theo squarely across the face.

What the hell was I supposed to look for?

Did he just start at the "D" section and flip through each hand-written card to look for a book titled "Death Runes for the Ignorant"? Did he need a dark witch's name to go find some tome with dried blood on it and just start taking notes? All of those intuitive investigation skills he relied on mindlessly like his own veins carried blood were all useless in the sheer amount of information available to him now. On top of that, the dormant magic filling the massive hall laid heavy on Theo's shoulders, looming over him as if waiting for the perfect trigger to be set off.

I'll have to start at the start.

The sudden burst of activity from the Black Staff coven, the ritualistic murders that led him to the consultant's door, the intricate drawing she gave that took him straight to the house of a murderous dark witch with green eyes and what seemed to be an earth pact... Surely there was a tome in here from a dead Black Staff member. They were too volatile and old to have gone entirely unnoticed by the SIA this long.

He wandered down the neat columns of wooden drawers—ordered alphabetically by subject instead of author, since most of these tomes probably didn't list the author's name—to thumb through the seven drawers in the "B" section until he came across his first read. Theo took note of the section and reference number for every card that mentioned anything about the Black Staff coven, twenty-six in total, before snapping his leather notebook closed and setting off on his research.

It was going to be a long, tedious night.

After many, many hours of ruffling through dusty pages and stacking old tomes beside him in a towering reject pile, he finally found the first inkling that he was not, in fact, losing his mind with this desperate research project.

It was in an old journal where he found the first mention of death runes. The slim book was soft to the touch, bound in hardcover with some kind of shimmering crushed velvet covering that seemed wholly impractical to protect contents of a magic variety. Most tomes owned by witches were rugged, leather-bound—or in unsavory instances bound with human skin—and bulky, with pages tattered and stained by use and age.

This one looked to be in pristine condition. The spine even cracked as if it had never been opened, though that had to be impossible judging by the little red flags bookmarking places for the SIA research team. Theo thumbed through pages of neat, evenly-spaced writing broken up by intricate technical drawings of ritual settings and rune analyses. Whoever authored this book was obviously well-studied and experienced in mentoring. Even for someone as magic-illiterate as him, the explanations of spells and the effects of certain elements and ingredients on spellcasting was incredibly digestible and easy to understand. It had the tone of a patient teacher who truly wanted the reader to connect and understand.

He flipped to the front in hopes it would give some clue who wrote this journal. There was no name, but instead a charcoal-drawn portrait of a woman from the shoulders up covering the entire front page. From the shading, it appeared her hair was dark, with slightly lighter shading of her skin indicating she was not wholly pale. Her chin—delicate and slightly pointed on her heart-shaped face—was tilted at a haughty angle, with thin lips topped by a pronounced cupid's bow pulled into a mischievous smirk. The woman had large eyes framed in full dark lashes that even in greyscale sparkled with that same mischievous light as her smile, with the telltale jagged lines of a thick shatter-pattern taking up the majority of her irises indicating she was a powerful witch. Whoever drew this even caught a slight wrinkle on the bridge of a pert nose as if it were crinkling in a playful way.

Was *this* who had written all these meticulous notes? Or was this a sketch of a loved one the author had drawn?

In the bottom right corner a signature was scrawled in a looping cursive, a messy counterpart to the neat writing on the other pages. Theo couldn't make out much beyond the two capital letters.

"D... G?"

Whoever this artist was, their talent was undeniable. The woman herself was very beautiful, someone who smiled easily and laughed often. He could see why the artist would want to immortalize her on paper. He wasn't well-versed in analyzing artwork, but there was something vaguely familiar about this drawing. Like trying to remember a childhood flavor, something tickled the back of his brain urging him to remember where he'd seen this before, or a piece like it maybe. Art as a whole was not widely displayed or celebrated, at least in his lifetime. Most people with artistic talents channeled them with magical mediums like rune calligraphy or ceremonial centerpieces used in elaborate rituals.

Where had I seen her before?

Before common sense could deter him, Theo gripped the top of the page and braced his other hand against the soft cover, and ripped the whole thing neatly from the front of the journal. He was sure a librarian somewhere just clutched their chest in shock with some uncanny sixth sense of appropriate book care. In a belated show of respect, he folded the drawing into a neat square and tucked it into the notebook at his elbow filling up with his research notes.

Just as he turned his attention back to the abused book, the very faint—but undeniable—shuffle of something across the stone floor froze every one of his muscles in place. In an intrusive thought, Theo wondered if the librarians who cared for these books like their children did in fact sense him ripping out the page, and were coming to take their pound of flesh.

Focus, Theo.

Theo checked the four-sided clock hanging from the center of the hall, so massive it was visible from all corners of the space. Just past nine o'clock... he had already been here over four hours. Surely, no one else was burning the midnight oil researching as well. Theo would have heard the heavy doors if anyone had come in or out. Just in case, he kept his ambient noise to a minimum and listened for any indication he wasn't alone anymore. It would be tough for him to explain away his own presence here; typically, detectives assigned this kind of work to the research team and waited for their reports back.

This time the sound was deliberate, a *chuff* of something soft skidding against the floor. At first he thought it was an idle sound from his own shoes, but not this time. He hadn't moved an inch, breathing lightly, ears straining, waiting to hear a sound that couldn't be him.

Someone was in the library with him.

It took a monumental effort for him not to curse aloud. It was unlike Theo to be sloppy and unintentional. Slowly, Theo shut the journal and lifted a few of the tomes up with both hands, placing the small book in between them to disguise the fact it was the last one he read. He wouldn't have time to put all these books away right now. He hoped whoever was here just popped in for a few minutes and he could get back to his work.

The visitor hacked wetly like something painful was caught in their throat, then they began wheezing on every inhale and exhale. That scraping sound echoed through the stacks, a little closer this time. Theo crept to the corner of the stack nearest the alcove he was camped out in and gently pressed his right shoulder against it as if to peek around it.

Then the *smell* hit his nostrils, and the intense urge to gag and retch almost blew his cover. Theo had to cover his mouth and pinch his nose with both hands to keep any sound from leaking out. Even then his eyes burned and watered, blurring his vision at the worst time. He only ever smelled something like this at gory crime scenes, particularly ones that were aged and rotten.

It was the smell of decaying flesh, mixed with some kind of chemical he couldn't place.

Who is in here with me?

Theo debated whether to risk being spotted by leaning over to see, but the decision was quickly made for him as the shuffling became faster and louder, like it was coming right toward his hiding spot. He moved away from the corner as quietly as he could and slipped behind the other end, back pressed against the solid wood of the stack as he tried to both control his erratic breathing and avoid gagging on the putrid smell.

A wet *thwack* shook the shelf he hid behind slightly. Snuffling and snarls started softly but grew louder with every second. It was the furthest thing from human-sounding. And it seemed dead-set on finding Theo alone.

His eyes shot to his right, to the precarious stack of tomes still sitting on the desk he was just at moments ago. The black spine of the journal he hid peeked out from between the others as if calling him to not leave it behind. That intuitive sense, the one that hadn't led him astray yet, told him the answers he was looking for were in that book.

I'm not leaving the journal behind after hunting for it for four long hours, even if a fucking monster is about to kill me!

The shelf shook again, more violently this time, books shifting and unsettling as whatever was on the other end seemed to run into it as it shuffled down the aisle to his right. It would see him in a matter of seconds.

Clenching his jaw, Theo stepped into the next aisle and yanked the black journal out from its stack, toppling the books above it and making a loud racket as priceless tomes fell to the stone floor. The thing let out a shrill scream—removing any doubt it was human with how impossibly high-pitched it was—and shoved the shelf like it was trying to knock the whole thing over onto Theo and crush him.

"Shitshit*shit!*" Theo ranted, throwing stealth to the wind as he ran to the safety of the main walkway, narrowly avoiding tripping on books that had toppled off the shelf as it was shoved again to a precarious angle. He dove out and rolled onto the red carpet that barely lessened the blow to his right shoulder and rib. Theo's breath was knocked from him as he struggled to gain his footing and run toward the exit, still clutching the journal like his life depended on it.

The shelf crashed into its neighbor, creating an awful domino effect of shelves falling and books toppling all the way down the row. Theo couldn't mourn the idea of someone walking in on this mess in the morning for long. His chaser—the one with the inhuman strength to topple said heavy bookshelf—was lumbering out from the aisle, and he was finally able to get a look at the creature.

Except it wasn't a creature at all. At least, not when he'd known her.

He narrowly avoided the swipe of Rebecca's hand as she reached for his shoulder, stumbling to the left on unsteady feet but far enough away to avoid another lunge. Her back was hunched and savage growls came from a mouth dripping some kind of pink-tinted fluid as her head bent toward the floor.

Theo backed away slowly, afraid any sudden movements would send her lurching after him again. He could barely keep the tears from his eyes seeing her body moving again. She was completely naked—which made sense since her body was probably in the morgue until the cremation ceremony—and the full extent of mutilation from the ritual was plain to see now. A ring of neat stitches wrapped around her throat, and beneath them the same runes that had been burned into the previous victim, now a harsh black against the deathly pale tint of her skin. Scrapes and cuts scattered across her back and down her left side as evidence of the fight she put up at the ritual site. The most gruesome desecration was the jagged slash across her lower abdomen that had also been stitched as carefully as the SIA research agent could manage.

Her uterus had been missing upon finding her body.

Rebecca twitched violently, as if puppet strings were being pulled to make her move. Her head flung back and arched her back at a painful angle as another piercing scream tore from her gaping mouth.

"What the fuck is going on?" Theo cried, breaths sawing in and out as he witnessed the worst kind of torture he could imagine. The kind that didn't end after death.

Her head whipped around, neck cracking at the sudden movement, and caught Theo in her soulless stare. Those were not the friendly brown eyes of the woman he looked up to as a mentor and friend. They were pitch black and unblinking.

His drastic flinch backward was enough to jolt her corpse into action. Her bare feet shuffled across the carpet faster than expected, leaving greasy smears on the floor as she lunged for him again. Specifically, it seemed she was lunging for the hand gripping the black journal.

"Rebecca!"

Another screech of frustration left her cracked lips. There was no Rebecca left in that shell.

Theo's hand—the one not clutching the journal—reached over to his shoulder holster to pull out the null pistol. He'd never heard of an agent taking out the undead with one of them, but maybe he could at least stun her enough to get a head start… and what? Was he going to leave this fucking corpse in the library for someone else to find?

Stuck in a moment of indecision, Rebecca snatched the wrist holding the gun with a slimy grip. Cursing violently, Theo yanked the hand—and gun—toward him while stepping to the left to throw Rebecca off-balance and slipped free, then lifted it high over his head and brought the butt down on the back of her skull on her way down.

The entire back of her head cratered, but nothing leaked out besides more of what he now realized was embalming fluid. Theo felt his gorge rise again in disgust.

Her body lay sprawled on the floor, arms sitting wherever they fell with no indication she even tried to break the fall. Theo lowered the barrel, aiming it under the left shoulder blade where a heart would be. But he hesitated again. Where could he shoot that would make a difference? There were no vital places left after the embalming.

She twitched again, fingers curling and uncurling. That made up his mind to shoot wherever the fuck he could put the nine bullets he had.

BAM! A shot to the heart.

BAM BAM! Another two to the head again.

BAM! One more bullet in the stomach.

Rebecca's body jerked with every shot as if she were alive, and that gutted Theo even more than he already was. It was like she was dying all over again, but this time it was his fault. How much more could his mind take before it snapped under the misery of losing someone else he cared about?

He let the tears trickle freely down his cheeks, paralyzed by the fear of moving his gun from her back and shock over the whole incident. The only sounds now were the ambient *tick, tock* of the clock now directly overhead and the erratic breaths he tried to control heaving from his chest. He counted the ticks, hardly blinking, staring at what seemed to be the once-again lifeless body of Rebecca Yarrow. Three minutes, and his arm shook from the tension of holding it up for so long.

She didn't move again.

"I'm sorry, Rebecca." His voice was barely above a whisper, harsh and full of emotion. Theo sniffled loudly. "I'm so fucking sorry this happened to you. I will find whoever it is and make sure this never happens again."

Even after being still for so long, Theo didn't turn his back to her body. Instead, he kept the gun in his hand and backed away slowly toward the exit, never taking his eyes off her until the heavy wooden door to the library shut between them. Then, he turned and bolted for the nearest emergency phone and picked it up to connect to the direct line for security.

"I need someone up in the library *now*," he demanded as soon as he heard someone pick up the line. "Like right fucking now! And bring some guns."

It only took the guards six minutes to gather backup and join Theo at the only way in or out of the library. But when one of them pushed open the right door and everyone stepped in behind her, there was nothing but the mess left behind from the shelves falling over down the right side of the hall. Where Rebecca had been laying, there was now a greasy pile of ashes in the rough shape of a body and the lingering smell of rotting flesh.

It took everything Theo had not to scream in rage at the loss of any evidence of what had happened. But it didn't smother the burning vengeance the encounter stoked in his chest. He *would* find the twisted, sick asshole who degraded Rebecca like this.

If it was the last fucking thing he did.

Chapter Ten

If Theo thought debriefing Captain Tate on his brush with a murderous witch was painful, sitting in his office mere days later to explain "what the actual holy fuck" he was doing in the library—the captain's words, not his—was more than unpleasant and highly interrogative. Especially since there was nothing but a pile of ash to indicate anything happened at all. In his experience, it was much harder to write a report without a body.

"It's highly convenient that the library—ergo the only place in the whole building we can't use magic without blowing up—is where this... thing decided to attack you." The captain rubbed his temples with his thumbs, elbows braced against the massive metal-and-glass desk he sat behind. He looked wholly fed up with this meeting, and it was only nine in the morning.

Never mind the fact Theo didn't sleep between the time he left SIA the night before and now. How could he, with the fresh memory of being attacked by his former partner haunting him every time he tried to close his eyes?

Killian glowered at him from under scruffy brows. "Start from the beginning again. What were you doing in there after hours?"

Shit. "I was looking for a book on runes." Not a lie. "Before Rebecca... died, she mentioned I could benefit from learning some simple tracker spells. I didn't really put much effort into studying before and could use some refreshing." Not a total lie, but definitely one of omission. If Killian found out *who* he was planning to track, he would yank his office access so fast Theo's head would spin. It was getting more and more difficult to keep the story straight under his observant stare.

"Hmmm..." he grumbled. "And you thought to do that at night, after I explicitly told you to take a few days off? Are you seeing how suspicious this makes you look?"

Theo knew the captain was giving him every opportunity to come clean, like a parent who suspected his child was lying but couldn't prove it, so he hoped Theo would fess up on his own.

Theo shrugged. "I don't know what else to tell you, sir. I didn't realize the library was closed at night."

"Just like you didn't know to sign in?"

Of course he would have checked the damn log. "It just slipped my mind. I didn't think that would throw my whole character into question after *being attacked by my undead partner.*" All he could do was lean into the victim play and hope for the best at this point.

Their eyes locked in an unspoken battle of wills, Killian trying to crack Theo's shell under the weight of his stare. He already knew this tactic from his fair share of interrogations. He kept his posture respectful but relaxed, his left leg crossed over the right and hands loosely clasped on his lap over his unbuttoned suit jacket with a blank and open expression.

Finally, Theo won the staredown. Captain sighed heavily, his shoulders drooping slightly. "Right. Well, needless to say you're still on administrative leave until this all gets cleared up. We're looking for a third party to come in and investigate, who specializes in this kind of... magic.. Or whatever the hell happened in that library. Honestly," he turned his head to gaze out the window, his voice thoughtful as he looked outside at the sunny morning, "just in my time here, it seems like practitioners get more power-hungry and corrupted. How far will these covens go? Sometimes I wonder how simple life must have been before humans had magic..."

"I wonder the same."

He grunted a non-committal sound. "Well, that's not the world we live in now, so we need to deal with this crisis. Without your help, Slater. I fucking mean it."

"Yes, sir."

Theo hoped the captain couldn't see the total insincerity of his answer. He just wanted to get the hell out of this office and away from the watchful eye of Killian Tate.

"Alright." Captain finally dismissed him, grabbing a stack of papers to tap against his desk as Theo's cue to leave. "Stop by HR on your way out to get the leave paperwork filled out."

Theo nodded, refusing to make eye contact on his way to the door with as minimal of a limp as he could manage. His back hurt on the best of days, but all the dodging and rolling around had caused old aches to flair back up as a brutal reminder Theo wasn't fully healed from his last brush with a witch.

Another two hours of filling out reports and paperwork with the dreaded Human Resources department, Theo felt weary to his bones as he pushed into his apartment and shut the door behind him, leaning back until his head rested against it and closed his eyes. Spending the morning being questioned by the captain and having to file redundant file after redundant file reliving last night was enough to wipe him out completely.

Even as mentally and emotionally drained as he was, Theo had a mission. He had a witch to find. The agency's witch. The one he was supposed to keep track of.

He sighed heavily.

Theo kicked his shoes off and tossed them by the door, an uncharacteristic show of carelessness compared to the rest of the shoes placed neatly on the three-tier shoe rack, organized by work shoes at the top and a row of running shoes along the bottom row. With singular focus, he moved through his home and into his bedroom. It was still a mess, not enough of a priority to clean up compared to the rest of the shitstorm this week had become.

The journal he snatched from the library had been a massive weight the whole way home, after the guards had come to find the ashes of Rebecca's reanimated body and sent him on his way. It had been small enough to slip into the inner pocket of his jacket, but with every minute he held it, the guilt that gnawed at his conscience had grown into a full-blown monster. By the time he stumbled in last night, he had thrown the journal into a small safe he had stashed in the corner of his walk-in closet, tucked behind some storage boxes of summer clothes.

If a coven of pissed-off witches—or even one pissed-off witch who had once owned this tome—decided to bust down his door and take it back, he doubted a measly old-school dial lock would deter them. He had found it in a store holding relics from before magic and bought the safe on a whim, and in his panicked and fatigued mind thought it was the best place to stash a magical book. Even touching it was a risk, since most of the tomes in that library had only been neutralized enough to pick up and read in the library. Who knew what would set this book off outside the SIA?

"I'm a fucking idiot."

Theo snatched a notebook and black pen off his desk and trudged over to the safe, still dressed from work, and set to unlocking it. As his fingers touched the dial, a shock tingled his fingers as if the dull metal was energized. An energy that had no business being there as it was a non-magic antique. The tome's magic, however docile it seemed, was very much active and affecting the safe.

His fingertips quickly became numb within the time of spinning the combination and pulling the small door open. While the book seemed small and innocent, sitting in the bottom of the small safe and blending in easily to the darkness it offered, a wave of foreboding rocked Theo's confidence as soon as he laid eyes on the velvety cover. The numbing tingle turned to icy shards stabbing through his veins and up his arm to the shoulder when Theo touched the book.

He hissed a curse but jerked his hand back out with his prize.

"Damn witches," seemed to be a constant mantra he repeated lately. Theo waved his hand at the light overhead to turn it on, trying to ward away the sense of dread that darkened his mood with its pale pink light as he opened the tome and his notebook to continue his research.

The pages fell open to the folded-up portrait he had ripped out of the journal from where he randomly jammed it in from his pocket. Theo unfolded the paper to reveal the mischievous woman's smirk, and with an impulsive thought set the picture aside where he could glance at it from time to time. Where the journal made his stomach twist with anxiety, her playful expression settled it like a cool glass of water. It was not entirely unlike the sensation he felt sitting on the other side of Dorianne's door, heart bleeding out on her porch, as she comforted him with her low voice and thoughtful words after Rebecca's death. Judging from the dates of each entry, it was impossible the drawn woman—if she was the author—was even alive. The journal was just over a hundred and fifty years old.

He had bigger issues to deal with, like finding the witch who could help him *now*, not a beautiful lady whose portrait he found in a witch's journal. Still, his eyes kept drifting back to hers, drawing him back to the knowing gaze of a woman he daydreamed he could find somewhere in this bleak world.

"I hope I find you, D. I need you."

Was that a wise choice, leaving the rat alive?

Dorianne stepped through the moving darkness of the forest, avoiding patches of light that filtered through the tree canopy with a wicker basket propped against her right hip. This was the most she had been outdoors in the last fifty years. The crisp freshness of the air was refreshing to her senses, a fizzy and pleasant burn in the back of her nose.

Dorianne snorted. Her displeasure of Theo's treatment—mainly, throwing his unprotected body off the balcony with intent to cause severe injury—was not unknown to the shadows. She was the one who swept his broken body away to land in the closest hospital after their callous actions. "What, you didn't do enough damage breaking several bones in his body?"

Well, we did warn him to leave.

"You could have easily ejected him from the house without the threat to his life."

Her own sentient shadows swirled around her body, leaving it free enough for her to reach out and pluck herbs and ceremonial ingredients with a pale, scarred hand. Tendrils snapped at the air in agitation. *Do you fear the agency will seek revenge for harming one of their own?*

"I'm not worried," Dorianne bent to pick some more wild herbs growing at the base of a massive oak. "Killian Tate will not let Theo follow me. He cares too much for the boy's life. And the SIA's subpar trackers will never be able to find me beneath my wards."

Damn straight, they won't, her shadows boasted. She could imagine them puffing their collective chest in pride. *There's something... different about that fool Theo, though. His aura had a certain flavor about him I can't put my finger on.*

"You don't have a finger."

They hissed. *Since when did you develop a sense of humor?*

The question struck a chord in Dorianne. She stopped on the narrow deer path she had been following back home, head bent toward the ground in thought. Other than empty acceptance of her fate, when *had* she last shown any kind of life? When had she been interested in something outside her wards? When had she even *laughed*?

The answer to all those questions was the same. When she reached out that first time to comfort Theo in his loss of his friend and mentor—a woman who had been her own handler for twenty years and not once spoke to—and for some insane reason thought it wouldn't end badly. He was a detective. Of course he would have been curious about her.

Although he was the one who broke through her wards, Dorianne was the one who baited him. She had shown him a sliver through the door, the possibility of a human on the other side of it, and he wanted to know more about her.

Dorianne had forgotten one important truth. She wasn't human. Not anymore.

And here I thought you were doom and gloom before. We're a conglomeration of demons from the pits of hell and have a brighter disposition than you do.

She swatted at a tendril that floated up to tickle her shoulder. "Sorry I can't be a ray of fucking sunshine. Oh wait, that would kill you!"

Dorianne continued along the trail, ignoring the spiny branches that grasped at her trailing black skirt and pulled at loose locks of hair that escaped the braid draped across a shoulder. In her dark mood, she welcomed the acute burning pain from walking through the scant rays of sun that pierced through the leaves, her own form of self-mutilation. Her companion, however, was very vocal about their discomfort at making them experience it with her.

Enough with the brooding! Jesus wept, you're less fun than an empty cemetery. And stop trying to take us down with you.

She stepped off the path and maneuvered through some more densely-packed trees, following the unique aura of her own magic from the wards to lead her back to the shaded clearing that hid the quaint cabin she tucked the dimension of her home into. The air around the log cabin immediately grew weighted with the power of the wards she had set. It was stifling even to her, the caster. Every time she stepped through the magic wall, it was like closing the door on her own cage.

Dorianne hated it.

She hated the hiding, and the lies, and the constant drain of magic taking its toll on her body and mind. Dorianne craved the human connection she once had, before she had to sever herself from her coven and the magic community as a whole. She sacrificed so much already. There was nothing else to give.

Basket laden with wolfsbane, belladonna, holly berries and wild lavender, Dorianne meandered through the sparse undergrowth of the shady clearing to climb the small porch and disable the wards to open the door. Now that she was in the middle of an unpopulated forest, she didn't need to worry about blending into a quiet suburb. Nothing was more suspicious than a house with no guests, or even worse, someone knocks by mistake and gets hit with a powerful memory spell to wipe away years of their life. Not exactly a neighborly thing to do. And she wasn't expecting anyone from SIA to come knocking, either.

Although she hoped...

I better not sense yearning coming from you, D, the shadows scolded her. *After we went through all that work to get rid of that pest, now you want him to hunt you down?*

She shot the ghostly form that had materialized behind her a nasty glare. "Could you get out of my head for five seconds?"

Impossible, unfortunately.

"*She* owes me, shackling some bitter harpies to my eternal soul. Can't a woman fantasize about a relationship in peace? God, go torment some spiders in the corner or something!"

Tsk, a sense of disgruntled acceptance eked from her shadow companion. *You have got quite the mouth on you now. We knew that man was a bad influence.*

Chapter Eleven

Dorianne's head jerked up, hands stilling over the mortar and pestle as something pricked her senses from beyond the clearing's ward.

No... it couldn't be.

A flurry of gray skirts and petticoats brushed across the floor. She pressed a shoulder to the frame of a window overlooking the area beyond the front porch and lifted the curtain the slightest bit with a twitch of a finger, trying not to be seen from the outside. The ward just beyond the shadowed glade rippled once, then twice. Almost like someone was... knocking.

Only one person was ignorant enough to think knocking on a witch's ward was appropriate. And from past experience, only one person would actually be able to touch it.

Him again? The shadows hissed over her shoulder as if looking out the window as well. *For Christ's sake, can't he take a hint? Next time I'll drop him in a layer of Hell, and we'll see if he makes it out of there in one piece.*

They sounded entirely too gleeful at that idea.

Sure enough, the chromatic sheen of the ward bowing inwards as if being pressed on the other side until a hand pushed through the center, followed by another hand. They turned outward, the backs pressed tight together, and pulled the ward apart like opening a curtain. It was an incredible feat to be sure. Dorianne didn't know whether to be impressed or immensely pissed off at the audacity.

Theo's upper body became visible next as he leaned forward to peer through the hole he made and look around the clearing. It seemed he learned from past mistakes—he obviously didn't want to get blindsided again. Maybe he wasn't a complete idiot after all.

Despite her annoyance, the tiniest smirk pulled Dorianne's lips up as she watched him creep through the ward. Seeing him made her incredibly giddy, for the first time in over two hundred years. Her companion scoffed at their shared emotional connection.

You're disgusting.

"Oh, shut up!" she hissed over her shoulder at her unwelcome commentator.

It took some serious effort to school her features to expressionless again and she marched over to the front door, throwing it open hard enough to bang against the porch wall and startle Theo. Dorianne stood in the entrance, arms crossed but feet firmly planted on her side of the threshold. She kept herself cloaked in darkness and out of sight.

"What in the actual hell are you doing here?" she called out. "You didn't get the hint I didn't want to be found? Should I have sent a letter of resignation?"

Despite her stern tone, Theo beamed in her general direction and shrugged. "I'm pretty stubborn when I want to be. But all the way across the ocean? Really? That's a bit drastic if you ask me. There's plenty of dark forests to brood on our side of the world. You know, the New States."

"That was kind of the point," she replied drolly. "I obviously didn't want to stay anywhere near Salem."

"Well you did a good job with that. It was a real pain in the ass to find you! No warm welcome?" He lifted his arms in a hug, which looked ridiculous from how far away he was. Like a puppy happy to see its owner return home, she couldn't help but feel a small sense of relief seeing him here.

"Is there a particular reason you're here? Since your ass was dealt some pain in the process?"

"I was worried about you."

"I am one of the most powerful witches alive! What is there to worry about?"

"Okay, maybe I also need your help!" Theo rolled his eyes dramatically and rocked back on his heels, slapping his hands against his thighs in frustration at her resistant behavior. "I don't know, Dorianne. Maybe I give a shit about you, okay? Now, can I come in, or do I have to keep yelling at a dark doorway? Also, I think I have something that belongs to you." His hand reached into a satchel she just noticed was slung across his chest as he pulled it forward to rummage around.

I can't let him in.

He'll see me.

What if I repulse him?

Dorianne drew her arms closer to her chest, more in response to intrusive thoughts than for actual protection. She knew what she looked like, how different she was to his very vital, very lively appearance. Her very existence was unnatural, even by magical standards.

Who cares if he likes your appearance? The shadows rebuked, obviously annoyed at her sudden self-consciousness. *He's the one showing up here unannounced and asking to come in. If he doesn't like how you look, he can fuck right off a tall cliff. We will gladly deal with him again. He won't be in enough pieces to deliver to a hospital this time.*

This decision felt pivotal.

"Does this look familiar?"

He held up something small, rectangular like a book, with a velvety sheen to it. As soon as she focused on it, her eyes prickled with tears from the sudden blast of nostalgia that slammed into her. She knew what it was just by the aura it emanated even from across the clearing.

It was her first tome. From when she was still a mortal, a young practitioner full of hopes and dreams for the future. The one that she had drawn in extensively.

"How..." Dorianne could barely string words together, she was so surprised. "Where... where in the world did you find that?" Dorianne suspected the witch who last held that book would have burned it to ash.

Theo shrugged casually, still holding the tome up high. "I don't know where it came from, but I found it in the SIA research library. I took it with me when—" He stopped himself, his gaze going somewhere else completely. "It's... a lot happened since you left. But this helped me come up with a tracking spell to find you. The stuff you wrote in here, it's incredible."

"A naïve girl wrote that tome," Dorianne explained. "Maybe it will help you figure out how to get back home too."

"D..." He moved closer to the porch, his sensible boots tramping through the sparse undergrowth but his eyes glued to the door. His brows pulled together in a pleading expression. "Come on. You kicked my ass once. It's not like I can actually hurt you, right? No one deserves to be alone forever."

"Like you're the expert on that issue. You have actively been pushing people away the majority of your life."

"And look where that's gotten me!" His cheeks puffed as he blew out a heavy sigh. "I just... see something in you. Something that's the same as me. Not literally, since I haven't actually seen you, but... I didn't realize how isolated I was until I started talking to you—"

"Charming."

He groaned in frustration. "I mean, my problems don't seem as impossible to deal with when I tell them to you. I don't feel as... bitter? Angry? At risk of sounding even more corny and desperate than I already do, you have made me a better version of myself just by being you, just by listening to me."

He's right, that was nauseatingly corny, the shadows agreed.

"Shut up," she whispered over her shoulder where they clung, giving their unsolicited opinion yet again. Then, she raised her voice to reach Theo, "So now what? You sweep me off my feet and whisk me away from my lonely existence? I cling to you as my hero and we live happily ever after?"

"No." He scoffed. "This isn't a romance book. But I'd like to start by coming inside and talking to you, face to face. Not having to talk through a door or yell into the void. I just want to get to know you, the real you. The witch that was brilliant enough to write a book like this to help ignorant people like me learn magic." He waved the black-covered book again. "Seriously, this thing is like 'Spellcasting for Dummies.'"

The disdain coming from her shadows was almost palpable. *Oh, please, spare me from this sad attempt at wooing you. Not a romance book, he says! Just shut the door and—*

Haven't I hidden for long enough? Dorianne's silent question was meek, but it stopped the rumblings of the demons' snarky commentary. *I shut myself away for two centuries, and everything I tried to avoid has come to pass as if it were inevitable. How much more regret must I carry? How many more lifetimes must I watch pass me by without a single emotional connection to someone else?*

The horde had no answer. Maybe they didn't even comprehend the starvation of human touch Dorianne had experienced as their vessel. But Theo was here, now, far away from the Black Staff coven, and Dorianne wouldn't let this opportunity pass her by.

Her confidence was bolstered by the earnest, eager look on Theo's open face. The darkness melted down her body and clung to her legs, trailing behind clinging to the floorboards in retaliation, as she took a large step over the threshold to stand exposed on the front porch. The demons' disgruntled mutterings started up again, but they slunk back even farther into the house until only a thready shadow connected them to her feet. Even with the bold decision to show herself, Dorianne crossed her arms tighter across the laced bodice of her dress and pressed her lips firmly together to keep a grimace at bay. The shade of the covered clearing wasn't incredibly bright, but still more than she was used to even under the porch's roof. Her eyes blinked rapidly and squinted until they could adjust to the dramatic change in lighting.

Dorianne's obvious discomfort had no effect on the overwhelming sense of awe Theo felt, meeting her face-to-face for the first time. His breath was sucked straight from his lungs at the shock of finally seeing Dorianne, alive and indignant with a cocky tilt to her chin.

She was the girl that ensnared him with those captivating eyes from the drawing, come to life. The page he had ripped out of the very tome in his hand. The one he carried around in his pocket even now. It was unbelievably surreal seeing her now, even as she scowled at him from the porch.

Wind teased the long, wavy locks of pure white hair that danced around a curvy waist cinched in with a simple gray bodice, covering her from the top of her neck down both arms to end each sleeve with black lace circling her wrists. What he could see of her hands tucked under the opposite elbows was incredibly pale skin stretched across long fingers, each tipped with black nails that seemed to naturally grow the color. His eyes continued downward across voluminous gray skirts in a similarly plain fabric to brush against the floor and offer tantalizing peeks of fluffy petticoats beneath the hem.

Finally, Theo's gaze traveled back up, up, up her statuesque height to admire the face he never in his wildest dreams would have imagined meeting in his life, but saw beauty in all the same.

Dorianne's eyes were the most startling in person, so bright they glowed like the sun itself shown through the thick shatter-pattern around her pupils. As he took another couple of steps forward unconsciously, he realized the irises were, in fact, two different colors, a golden yellow in the center that blended into the verdant green of newly-grown grass around the very edges. Such fantastic colors seemed a stark contrast to everything else about her that was pale and monochromatic. The skin across her face was absolutely littered with scars that were obviously not her own doing, from their jagged cuts reaching to her ears from the corners of her mouth and raised ridges scattered along the upper and lower lips, as if... they had been sewn together, or otherwise brutally sealed, and then ripped apart.

She unfolded her arms to fidget with her hands, wringing them nervously in front of her. "So... are you coming in? The sun is hurting my eyes. And give me my tome back already."

"Yeah..." was his dazed reply as he moved to climb the porch steps. With every foot closer, she became more and more mesmerizing, like the pattern of a butterfly's wings coming into focus. She held out a hand as if to take the book from him, her brow wrinkled in consternation as if she considered slamming the door in his face. Slowly, as if to savor every moment she reached out to him, he placed the book in her waiting palm but didn't let go as she grabbed it.

He was a bit sheepish to admit the page he stole. Theo figured he'd be better off coming clean now, before she opened it. "I, uh, ripped out the drawing in the front. Sorry. I just... it's a really nice picture. I had no idea it was of you."

The admission so freely given caught her off guard. Lost for words, Dorianne just shrugged it off. "Keep it. Like I said, this tome was written by a naïve girl. I barely know her anymore."

She moved to the side to let him through the door, following him inside and pulling it shut behind her. The room was immediately thrown into a cozy kind of darkness, the only source of light a small fire lit in the stone fireplace. It was sparsely furnished—only a couple of faded green armchairs facing the fireplace, a low live-edge wooden table made of some kind of light wood that seemed to have been taken straight from a tree with some legs put on it, and a simple mantle above it—but very cave-like and soothing.

"Do you want something to drink? Tea? Water?"

"Tea is fine. No poison, right?"

Her lips pursed, trying to maintain an expressionless façade but failing miserably. "Not yet. It is my own blend, though, so it may be just as bad."

"Color me shocked! Dorianne Grey admitting she is bad at something?" Theo gripped his chest with both hands in a dramatic gesture. He could tell the smile was almost breaking through her wall of social insecurities.

"I'm good at the things that matter."

A mischievous grin lit Theo's face and he pretended to look her over appreciatively. Dorianne rolled her eyes and moved toward the small galley-style kitchen, her skirts brushing against his pants as she walked by. She set the tome gently on the kitchen counter that stretched between them and separated the living room space.

"Pray tell, what are those 'things that matter?'" Theo curved his fingers in air quotes.

"Most of them involve someone dying." She turned and narrowed her eyes at him. "Stop grinning like that, it makes you look feral."

"What, showing my teeth? That's what offends you?"

"You looking that giddy offends me."

"I love this prickly side of you. Although I guess it's not surprising you have one." Theo leaned his hip against the counter of the quaint kitchen, a warm feeling budding in his chest watching her light a fire beneath a kettle of water with a flick of her fingers. "Can I help with anything?"

She huffed. "Just stay out of my way. This kitchen is small." One of her hands waved in his direction, indicating the natural wood cabinet behind his right shoulder. "Grab the tea cups and saucers from there and put them on this tray."

As she spoke, a silver tray nudged open another cabinet door and floated to land gently on the counter between them. He could tell she was trying her hardest to keep her eyes on anything but him as she bustled around, pulling canisters and silverware and other accouterments to add to the server tray. It was oddly endearing.

Theo didn't want to be turned into a plump toad or whatever other twisted punishment she could come up with, so he turned to collect his assigned cups and placed them on their saucers. He carried the tray into the living room and placed it on the rustic coffee table before sitting himself. Just like Dorianne, they were beautiful in their simplicity from the outside, stark white china with dainty handles and no pattern on the surface. On the inside, however, was an intricate black lacy pattern originating from the very bottom and climbing up the walls to the rim. Classy and understated.

The owner of the china was much more complex and interesting to Theo.

He lounged casually on the green loveseat, his head propped in a hand. Leaning against the armrest, he watched Dorianne with what could only be fascination. She was still studiously avoiding his eye, fully devoted to carrying the teapot by its black handle with another scarred hand cupped underneath the stout body. Everything about her was a study in effortless grace.

The white braid holding her hair back slipped over a shoulder when she bent down to pour their tea—not spilling a single drop—and set the pot to the side.

"Honey? Milk?" She stayed where she was, bent over the coffee table opposite to Theo and waiting for his answer.

"Neither."

Without a reply, she lifted a saucer to Theo, and that's when he saw it. The slight tremor in her hands. The china teacup, completely unforgiving, clattered the slightest bit on its saucer as it shook. Dorianne was nervous. Maybe even scared.

One of Theo's hands reached past the china to cup one of her hands gently, and it clattered hard enough to shift the little spoon from its resting spot. The fingers of his other hand wrapped around the edge of the saucer to cradle it in his own grip and pull away. Left without anything to hold, Dorianne's cool fingers slipped into his rough palm and he closed his fingers around the long bones of her own.

"Come sit with me."

Finally, slowly, she lifted her eyes from the cup to meet Theo's. So close, the color was breathtaking and unique and vibrant against the washed-out color of her skin and the somber shades she dressed in. Like the color had been sucked out of every other part of her except for them. Lost in her captivating stare, Theo failed to notice the shadows around her take the form of a giant snake until it slithered up her back and over her left shoulder, its head a massive triangular shape with glowing red eyes that leveled on him disdainfully. It flicked a dark tongue out and opened its mouth to reveal massive fangs before hissing viciously.

"Shit!" He pressed into the corner of the couch, knees pulled up to his chest and both hands gripping the sofa. "When the fuck did you get a snake?"

Her eyes rolled before cutting a scathing side eye to the snake. "I didn't. Apparently, becoming a burden for all eternity is not enough for the horde of demons I'm bonded to, now I have to suffer gaining their approval to not throw you to the wolves."

The snake's eyes narrowed slightly.

"Wait…" Theo's brain whirred, trying to put the pieces together from his last encounter. "This… these can take any shape they want? Is this what I saw in your house in Salem?"

HISSSS!

Theo took that for a yes. "You're a real asshole, you know that, Shady? I could have done without being thrown off a damn balcony and ending up in a hospital! If I had known I had to deal with you again, I would have brought a fucking lantern," he grumbled and crossed his arms.

There was a tense moment of staring between Theo and the snake. Its mouth opened to give him another hiss, but Dorianne broke the silence with a bright peal of laughter. Tears formed in the corners of her crinkled eyes. "Sh-Shady? Shady! Oh, Jesus wept I cannot..." Her sentence deteriorated into another string of laughing and the snake slowly turned its head to glare at her.

I cannot believe the level of disrespect you mortals think you can show the demonic horde of Azazel! I could drag you to the pits of Hell to be ripped apart for all eternity until the very shreds of your pathetic soul are—

Dorianne swatted a hand at the snake's head, causing it to dissipate like fanning away a foul smell before it reformed again. "Don't listen to them. Shady is just a sore loser and even sorer company." She was still gasping for air and trying in vain to recover from her boisterous hysterics at the horde's expense.

The disembodied response was mostly hissing. *If you start calling me that, I swear to the Dark Lord I will—*

"Do nothing."

Growls rumbled from the darkened shadows, but the shadows seemed to admit defeat as they slunk behind the couch Dorianne and Theo sat on. *Stop interrupting me, you hag!*

The unease clearly broken between them, Dorianne picked up her own saucer and moved around the table to sit beside Theo as Shady continued to grumble and grouse from behind the couch. His own cup—abandoned in light of his abrupt introduction—floated toward him from the general vicinity of the floor. "I caught this, in case you still wanted some tea?"

The cup was perfectly preserved, not a single drop on the saucer indicating it had even been disturbed. "Wow... uh, thank you. Yes, I would have been sad to waste tea."

Petulantly, Shady slithered off to merge with the abundant amount of dark corners in the otherwise cozy cabin. Just watching the shadows move so realistically sent a chill down Theo's spine—he hated snakes. And he now wondered if Shady somehow knew that when it chose its form.

Dim purple fire danced in the fireplace and served as the only source of light in the room. Dorianne kept her attention on the flickering flames as she sipped her tea, recovered enough to attempt being casual with having Theo in her home. "So, tell me," she cleared her throat of her voice's raspiness, then tried to speak again, "How did you manage to track an untraceable witch? I'm assuming there's not an army of SIA agents lurking in the forest as backup."

Theo snorted a laugh and sipped his own drink. "It's all thanks to your tome, actually. You have a real gift for explaining spellcasting for someone like me to be able to understand. I just followed the section on adapting tracking spells to my specific situation."

"It doesn't work like that, Theo. You can only use that magic if you have the capacity for it." She gestured to his eyes, thin cracks of black shattering the warm hazel of his irises. "Judging from your pattern, you are capable. So, something is holding you back."

Theo kept his lips pressed tightly shut.

Dorianne hummed. "And you totally trusted the book of a witch you didn't know to not have malicious intent? I could have called those spells tracking but actually been suicidal." Her face was expressionless, but he could see the tension begin to build in her shoulders as she spoke—practically berating Theo. He already knew she was going to lose it at his next answer. Dorianne didn't fool him with her blank façade; there were vicious undercurrents swirling beneath that smooth surface, and he was about to receive the brunt of a tidal wave's worth of anger.

"I just... had a good feeling. Whatever magic clinging to that tome reminded me of you."

Theo was right. She did lose it.

Dorianne slammed the saucer and cup down on the coffee table, shattering both to pieces and cracking the edge off the table before bolting upright off the couch. Finally, she looked down her nose to meet Theo's eyes again, and the disbelieving rage in them could have set him on fire.

"Where is your sense of self-preservation?" Her voice was thundering, loud enough to make the rest of the china tremble where it sat. "How completely inept and ridiculously stupid are you to just start playing with magic like an imbecile? I cannot even..." There were no other words she could muster, but she sputtered angrily and stormed off to the kitchen to leave Theo sitting in her residual emotion. He stared at the sad, broken china and wood scattered across the hardwood floor in thoughtful silence.

Eventually, he mustered the courage to put his saucer down and follow Dorianne.

She stood in the corner, hands braced against the countertop. Her shoulders drooped heavily, rising and falling with the intentionally slow breaths she took to calm herself. Dorianne's head hung down low, her braided hair still draped over her shoulder to expose a line of jagged-looking runes etched into the pale skin, starting at her hairline and scrolling down over each bump of her elegant spine. Theo knew what they were just at a glance—death runes.

"Dorianne..." His voice was little more than a murmur. He lingered by the open door, worried that approaching her now would make her feel trapped.

Her reply was just as quiet, but no less emotional. "You could have died."

"But I didn't."

"You had no business casting spells with your level of experience."

"I needed to find you."

"Right..." Another shuddering sigh shook her. "To ask about the runes."

"No."

It was a simple enough answer, but the meaning held so much more. Theo didn't need Dorianne for what she knew about dark magic. He didn't need her to solve his parents' murder. He needed her for that comforting presence that belonged only to Dorianne Grey. For the steadfast confidence she exuded. For the grace she seemed to navigate life with. For the caring nature she showed now, hidden under all those layers of bitterness and holding the world at arm's length.

She finally turned. There were no tears wetting her cheeks, but the distraught look on her face was enough to pull him across the kitchen and pull her into a tight hug. At first, her body tensed as if electrocuted, hands clenched into the skirts at her thighs. But Theo just held her tighter and buried his face into the crook of her neck to breathe her in.

"I just need you."

Chapter Twelve

It felt like he'd stood there for hours, wrapped in the chill of Dorianne's skin and mellow, earthy scent. Theo felt like he was buried beneath the dark, rich soil of the forest, breathing in the petrichor with herbal notes woven through it. He could hardly believe her body was substantial, that someone like him could be standing here now and holding her in his arms. Ever so slowly, she turned her body in his hold. Her arms moved beneath his, lifting and hesitating in the air until they finally wrapped around Theo's waist. Those long fingers twisted into the fabric of his jacket like she was worried he would pull away.

Theo lifted his head to graze his lips along the skin of her neck, every second an eternity as he constantly checked with Dorianne's nonverbal signs that he was about to get lit on fire. A shaky exhale rattled from her chest and she pulled away slightly to meet his eyes. The war between home and reluctance darkened those golden-green eyes as they flicked between his own, mouth beginning to open just the smallest bit with a small gasp. He was worried his breath trembled too much out of fear and excitement.

Gently, so gently, his soft lips brushed against hers. Just the barest touch burned as if he had frostbitten skin shoved under hot water. That's how intense and concentrated her magic was. He could only imagine what miracles she could bring to life.

He was shocked to feel her reciprocate, eagerly pressing her own lips back against his as her cold hands crept around his waist and up over his pecs, inching up until they clasped onto his shoulders in a tight grip. As her fingers skirted the healed stab wound they sparked slightly, the snapping sound startling them both out of their momentary daze.

"What was that?" Her brow crinkled in concern, chest still rising and falling with every heated pant.

"Just something stupid I did." Theo pulled her close and bent slightly, gripping her behind the thighs to lift her up onto the counter so he could push between her knees. Their height difference was negligible now, but he could sense her excitement pressing this close to him, being this open and vulnerable.

Dorianne's eyes searched his own as if waiting for him to bolt out of the door. When he didn't make a move to shake her grasp, she leaned even closer to study his face in awe. "You're so warm. And your aura, it's mesmerizing. I feel so... light."

Theo smiled under her lips that had reconnected to his own. "So I'm not a total menace?"

"Oh, you are definitely still a menace." Dorianne pressed light kisses up his jawline, leaving a burning trail in their wake that set his pulse racing. "But you're tolerable now, I suppose. Or my magnanimity has gotten much stronger." The black nails tipping her fingers pierced straight through Theo's thick jacket and shirt and pricked his sensitive skin. The burning, the nails, and her freezing body chilling him were almost over-stimulating.

Dorianne lifted her hands to bury long fingers in his dark waves. They gave a teasing pull that went straight to his cock as if she had pulled it on a puppet string, bucking enthusiastically in his jeans. She chuckled at his responsiveness.

"Show me," she cooed in his ear and caught the lobe in teeth that felt just the slightest bit too sharp. "Show me how to feel like a woman seduced by a man. Show me how you drive a woman senseless with lust."

Theo scoffed, trying not to blow his load just by listening to her smoky voice. "Jesus, D. If I had known you could talk like that, I would have tried scrying you more." Her throaty chuckle brought the biggest smile to his face and he pressed it into the curve of her neck, trying to hide how giddy he was just being this close to her.

"Your sarcastic banter is one of my favorite things about you." She nipped his ear one more time. "Well, up until now. I'm hoping whatever you're hiding in these pants tops that list. I can't wait to find out."

His hands rucked up the grey skirt to reveal long, almost translucent-pale legs hidden among the voluminous petticoats. Theo's fingertips bumped along ragged scars that littered almost every inch of her skin, silvery and almost invisible to the eye but told a life of violence and surviving to those who she let close enough. A pained expression pulled the corners of his lips down slightly, not heavy enough to wipe it away entirely but enough for Dorianne to notice.

"I've lived a long life, Theo." Her thumbs brushed reassuringly against his temples, the fire in her eyes no less bright but her face soft in kindness. "My scars are not something to pity. They are proof that I overcame everyone who sought to destroy me."

"You're... incredible," he breathed. "And gorgeous. God, I can't wait to be inside you."

Desperation made him impatient, struggling against the many layers of her skirt until they were all bunched up around her waist. Her boisterous laugh only emboldened him to hoist her up higher and press her harder against the wall as he struggled with the skirt's many underlayers.

"Jesus wept, do you have enough fucking layers on? I'm drowning over here," Theo grumbled but moved his hands to her ass. His eyes widened and shot back up to hers. A coy smirk was on her lips now.

She wasn't wearing underwear. Dorianne was walking around bare this whole time. Theo was going to have a stroke from the blood rushing to his head and lighting his cheeks up in a frenzied blush.

"You were saying?"

"Shit!" Now he was very motivated. "Unbutton me. Get me out, out!"

She taunted him. "Is this how the handsome, rugged Theo Slater charms all his women?"

Theo shuddered hard when the backs of her fingers slipped between his skin and the jean fabric, and she ran them back and forth along his waistband a few times, knowing it would drive him wild. Goosebumps prickled along the taut skin of his abs in response.

He was done with her teasing. In jerking movements, Theo set her on unsteady feet and spun her roughly to yank on the strings holding her corset tight. Amidst the muttered curses and panting he finally managed to loosen it enough and pulled the dress over her head with it, throwing her clothes carelessly on the floor. The warmth of a hand pressed between her shoulder blades and Dorianne leaned over the counter. The *thud* of his knees hitting the floorboards hard heightened her excitement, and Dorianne bit her bottom lip to hold in a moan when he pulled her hips back even more to.

He didn't say a word, but soft hair brushing her inner thighs gave away his intent seconds before the warmth of his wet tongue glided along her folds, burning in the most titillating way and driving her mad with emotion she hadn't allowed herself to feel for decades. Theo completely ravaged her like he was half-crazed with starvation. Every moan from his mouth vibrated through her core and made everything clench in response.

"God, Theo," she practically wailed, reaching both hands out in front of her to dig her nails into the wood of the counter she was pressed against. Even the shadows that usually drifted peacefully around her legs were writhing wildly. "I c-can't... oh, God... *ugh!*"

His arms wrapped around her waist just as her body went limp from the earth-shattering orgasm he wrought from her in just seconds.

"I'm not done with you yet." Theo's expression turned almost feral with lust as he pressed impossibly closer to her, nudging her pussy with the tip of his cock. Dorianne hadn't even noticed when he stripped out of his pants because she was so out of her mind with unbridled emotion. One hand reached up between her chest and the counter and gripped her chin firmly, turning it far enough over her shoulder to capture it in a devouring kiss and swallowing the gasp that slipped out as he thrust roughly into the most intimate part of her. The stretch, the smooth glide, the feeling of Theo filling up every hole stabbed into her soul from a painfully long existence, caused tears to pool in the corners of her eyes and trickle over her nose to pool beneath her left cheek.

He understood what they were for. Theo's lips peppered kisses along Dorianne's flushed cheekbone to brush against the sensitive shell of her ear. Lodged this deep inside her, Dorianne would be surprised if he couldn't feel the very hammering of her heart.

"Dorianne..." His voice was tender despite the brutal intrusion. "D... you're the most incredible miracle I've ever known. I can't even—" Theo moaned, frustrated with his inability to tell her just how much she changed his life.

Dorianne's palms cupped his face. The most empathetic smile he'd ever seen on her small lips made his jumbled emotions rise up from his chest to lodge in his throat.

"Thank you," was all she could think to say in reply. "Now *show* me how you feel."

The fragile moment was broken. "With pleasure."

Theo pulled back to just the tip, then slowly drove his cock back through the welcoming slick walls until his hips met hers again. Then he rocked back and forth a few times before pulling back out again. The slow, irregular rhythm quickly became maddening for Dorianne.

"Faster! Please!"

"Hmmm..." He nipped at her throat lightly. "I do like to hear you beg." But Theo didn't oblige, dragging his cock out to the very end again. He was waiting for her next move.

"Please, fuck me faster! Please, please, please..." She could hardly believe the sound of her own neediness, making her voice this thready and vulnerable. As if to counterbalance sounding so weak, she dug her claw-like nails further into the wood, deep enough to leave deep scratches as she pulled her hands back.

"This isn't fucking, D," Theo growled. "This is way more. You're. *Never.*" Thrust. "*Getting.*" Thrust. "*Rid.*" Thrust. "*Of me.*"

Now that he had sped up to her liking, Theo's hands cinched around her waist tight enough to dent the skin. If she were able to bruise, he would have left them. As it was, her hips was slamming against the counter's edge with every jarring thrust and her eyes threatened to roll back with the sensory overload. His heat. His breath skimming across her collarbone. Droplets of sweat dripping from his temples and landing on her back.

It was all too much, and everything she ever wanted.

Darkness swirled up from the floor in a chilling vortex, encasing the two in a world of their own void of any light or sound beyond their cries and growls of passionate release. Frost formed on Theo's face where a fine sheen of sweat glistened just moments before and his body shuddered violently on its last thrust into her body, tensing from the severe cold and bucking of his cock in equal measure.

Chattering and hissing echoed around them from the bodiless creatures who lived in the shadows that clung to Dorianne.

"Is Shady commentating?" Theo asked, half amused and unsettled at the idea of voyeurs. Still holding Dorianne tightly against his hips, he rested his forehead on her shoulder as he tried to slow his racing heart and ragged breathing.

Dorianne's laugh was as light as the fingertips that brushed along the nape of his neck. "More like cheering. They are living vicariously through my sexploits."

Theo snorted. "Is that what we're calling this? A sexploit?"

"I'm very noncommittal. Almost allergic to commitment, really."

"I'm sure I will have a ton of competition beating down your door, in the middle of this creepy ass forest in the middle of nowhere."

"A girl can dream."

Carefully, Theo pulled himself from Dorianne and steadied himself against her, draping himself over her back as they caught their breath together. Slowly, the shadows encompassing them dissipated like petals dropping from a rose, letting in the warmth of reality and chasing away Dorianne's signature chill.

"Bath?" he asked in a husky voice.

"Only if it's with you."

His lips curled into a smile and opened to give a cheeky response, when an ungodly clap of sound broke through the post-coital haze and shook the windows in the kitchen almost to shattering.

Chapter Thirteen

K^{*sshhh-BOOM!*}

The cabin shook with the massive shockwave that followed what sounded like lightning striking just outside. The front door shook on its hinges, rattling in the door frame with every consecutive hit as they increased in frequency. Theo, who had been halfway to pulling Dorianne upright, nearly dropped her in shock as his head whipped toward the door. She stumbled back to brace against the counter again.

"The hell is that?"

Dorianne sighed wearily, but seemed mostly unconcerned. She stepped around him to pick up the topmost layer of her dress—forgoing the hassle of the undergarments and corset—to slip back over her head with an disturbing lack of urgency. "Some unwanted guests are trying to break my wards, it seems."

"And... we're not panicking about this?"

"No."

He was baffled by her utter lack of concern. "Can I ask why?"

Another deafening *BOOM* answered him, shattering the single window over the sink on the adjacent wall and making Theo flinch to cover his face. It was almost like the ward was being strategically attacked at certain points along its boundary. He scrambled to pull his pants back into place and button up, grateful he didn't have to get completely redressed before hurrying to follow her through the living room.

"Because I am about to, as you would say, fuck someone up."

Shady chattered from the corner they were lurking in—the distinct sound of teeth gnashing and claws clicking together coming from the culminating darkness that seemed to expand and contract as if breathing—far away from the threat of any light that might sneak through the breaking windows. As she walked by toward the front door, they caught the hem of her dress and gathered around her lower body in a billowing cloud, climbing up her body in snaking tendrils to wind down her arms and across her torso.

Theo followed her, wary of the dark mood she was in. "Don't you have issues with the daylight?"

"Not where I'm planning on standing."

Now Theo was *extremely* baffled. Was she trying to get herself killed? And what the hell was he going to do against a coven of pissed-off witches if she did die? He didn't exactly pack for a full-blown war out here in the middle of an Irish forest. The sight that greeted him as he joined Dorianne on the covered porch made his hand twitch for his piddly null-magic pistol.

Bodies three rows deep lined the perimeter of the outermost ward. Given the area it covered, there had to be at least a hundred witches surrounding the clearing, all with glowing hands and mouths uttering spells in an attempt to get through. All their eyes were glowing an ominous red.

One woman stood out in the back, lurking far beyond the line of practitioners ringing the perimeter, covered in a heavy black cloak with a deep hood. Even from the far distance, Theo could see the crimson of her eyes as they pulsed and thick black veins stretching across her cheeks and temples, and once their gazes locked he felt frozen in place. Like prey caught in the sight of a predator.

A predator he sat in front of in Rebecca's home, a wolf in sheep's clothing as she allegedly healed him after the witch's attack. A woman who looked eerily similar to Dorianne, now that he had seen them both. So similar they could be sisters.

This was all a trap!

Theo turned to warn Dorianne when every muscle in his body locked up, and the old gash in his side blazed to life as if a branding iron had been pressed against it. A pained scream was muffled behind clenched teeth as fire ripped through his veins. He was totally paralyzed, not even able to crumple to the ground.

"Theo?" Now Dorianne sounded concerned. "Theo, what's wrong? Let me–"

The next second brought with it fiery chaos.

Something exploded from inside Theo, a massive ball of magic with a bloody crimson aura, and shot outward, slamming Dorianne hard enough against the porch railing to break and send her sprawling on the grass. As soon as the spell left his skin, Theo crumbled to the porch floorboards, unable to do more than barely open his eyes to watch the worst possible outcome in this situation.

The spell expanded until it pressed against Dorianne's ward from the inside, melting it away in a sparking battle between the two magics before the shield dissolved completely and the hostile spell dissipated into thin air. Everyone was silent. Even the forest seemed to hold its breath in the face of what just happened.

Dorianne was the first to break the silence as she pushed herself off the ground. She had just barely avoided the direct sunlight where she landed beneath the overhang of the roof, but blisters bubbled on one pale foot that had the misfortune of landing in direct sun as it sizzled like cooking meat.

"*Shit!*"

A hysterical chorus rose all at once, the voices of all the witches clashing together to finish their spellcasting before she could recover. Shady expanded to a billowing cloud of shimmering darkness that enveloped Theo and Dorianne, absorbing the spells being thrown from every direction as she pulled herself off the ground and stormed across the meadow. Dorianne's eyes were locked on one person only, and not even the threat of deadly magic being hurdled at her or the limp caused by a severely burned foot would distract the burning hatred that fueled her.

"*Dylan!*" The roar that burst from Dorianne's snarling lips was terrifying and inhuman, as if the shadows she were bonded to had fully possessed her. "*You fucking spineless bitch! Come face the monster you created!*"

The witch in the back, seemingly the one responsible for bringing the barrier down, flung her arms out to either side and fell back to be swallowed by some kind of portal she had created. An eerie, tinkling laugh filled the once-peaceful meadow, reaching Dorianne's ears even over the screams of the Black Staff witches as they continued to barrage her with their useless spells. A bottomless void pulled the cloaked body of Dorianne's cowardly sister through and closed behind it as if she was never there.

"Fucking Dylan!" Dorianne spat like an angry cat. Shady blasted out from her body, knocking over the closest arc of enemies and shooting into the sky like a inky fountain. The shadows spread to envelop the immediate clearing around them in an artificial night. A black curtain made entirely of magic fell between Dorianne and the front lines of the coven, not nearly as wide as the original ward but still substantial-looking. Heavy thuds muffled by the barrier carried through the small space as witches on the other side barraged it with spells.

"How did she manage to get through? Did she..." Her eyes now glowed their own verdant green as they shot down Theo's prone body. Pieces fell into place as her gaze narrowed to slits. "Of course. She used *you*. Did you know you were carrying a ward-breaking curse? Were you working with *her*?"

As she spoke, Dorianne's voice grew deep and menacing, more animal than human. Her black nails had lengthened to veritable claws and the fingers stretched to extend their reach even farther. Every angle in her face grew impossibly sharp, the skin pulled taut against the bone beneath and hollowing out the spaces of her cheekbones and eye sockets. White hair whipped around in a vortex that seemed to originate with her rage. Her injured foot was completely forgotten at this point, healed over to make even more scarred flesh on her body.

Dorianne... Shady's striated voice called to her. *Interrogate the human later. I cannot last much longer like this.*

Her answering snarl made Theo wince. His arms were as feeble as a newborn's when he struggled to sit up on knees and elbows, still curled in a ball of residual agony from the spell's effects. Theo rested his forehead against the floorboard to catch his breath.

Shadows remaining from the makeshift barrier pooled beneath her feet and trailed behind in a growing train that rippled like fine silk as it drifted across the ground. Dorianne lifted her arms slowly, the living shadows rising with them to create a smaller bubble of darkness around her body, completely opaque from the outside. It closed at the top just as the outer barrier burst apart in a deafening explosion. The witches attacking it were brutally knocked back, thrown into each other and nearby trunks with their bodies strewn around the clearing's perimeter.

The surface of her personal barrier began to... ripple. Like a pebble being thrown across the smooth surface of a deep, dark lake. Theo had no idea what was going on, but the hostile witches apparently did. Almost as one they threw their hands up and chanted frantically, the glow from their hands becoming so bright it challenged the sun itself and he had to squint his eyes against it. That same oppressive weight Theo came to recognize as Dorianne's magic pressed down on the clearing, so heavy it was difficult to even breathe. Another wall formed between her and the coven, this time a rosy pink as it bridged from witch to witch and stretched up toward the tops of the trees. With every painfully slow second the wall was built, the chanting grew louder and faster, seeming to urge it to hurry.

"*Alazk kemasult brekshen, petchlak jask tak fentchimask.*"

The language was nothing like Theo had ever heard in his life. It seemed to come from the sphere of shadows encasing Dorianne, but surely, her voice wouldn't be able to sound as grating and jagged as that. Whoever spoke like that would ruin their vocal chords on the impossibly harsh edges of it. But in response, the ball shrank around her, leaving behind grotesque limbs with clawed tips and giant hands holding some particularly brutal-looking weapons dripping in black ichor as the darkness shrank more and more to fit Dorianne's body.

Theo could only watch on in horror, cheek pressed to the floor, as demonic monsters seemed to be birthed from the inky sphere that had once surrounded her.

Her moniker as Mother of Shadows took on a whole new meaning now.

Demons scattered throughout the clearing, cleaving down anything that had the misfortune to catch their eye. Whatever spells the coven threw at them seemed to have no effect, magic sinking into their skin like it had been absorbed to fuel their own strength. It was the screams of the dying that finally propelled Theo up off the floor, every movement a burning sensation to his nerves as if he'd been lit on fire from the inside. His newfound skill of ward breaking didn't have much of a purpose here, but he felt driven to try and stop this bloodbath Dorianne had started.

His throat felt parched. "Dorianne..." The feeble voice Theo mustered barely made it past his lips, lost in the cacophony of wails. He gripped the banister with both hands to hold himself up on shaking legs. Whatever that curse was, it had completely sucked him dry of energy almost to the point of unconsciousness. Even now, he could barely keep his eyes open as he sagged over the remaining banister railing like an old rug left out after a good beating.

Stairs were going to be an issue.

Demonic-looking creatures continued to pour from the massive globe of shadows Dorianne created, floating above the ground as it shrank smaller and smaller with each separation. Within seconds, the watery darkness clinging to her body curled in the center like a newborn baby in the womb. Any spell that happened to break through the writhing masses of demons and witches battling just flickered out against the second skin. It could have been absorbed, or completely nullified.

Theo had no way of knowing if she was affected in this state. His body was beginning to come alive again, every movement lagging as his muscles spasmed and retaliated against his brain trying to push them into action. Shakily, he pushed himself up from his slumped-over position and stumbled to the stairs, gripping the handrail with both hands as he tried his best to hurry down the steps and go to Dorianne.

The success was short-lived as his foot caught on a hidden rock and sent Theo sprawling into the shin-high grass. Never in his life had he felt more weak and pitiful as he did now.

A deafening shockwave blasted across the clearing, strong enough to throw clumps of dirt and rocks and displacing roots. The sheer force of the blast formed a crater beneath Dorianne that she now hovered even farther above with the ground now just...gone. Anyone who had been on their feet—minus the demons—had been knocked to the ground and scattered among the trees. She uncurled with her head thrown back and hair flicking like a cape spun from moonlight behind her. In her outstretched hand, wisps of shadow culminated and solidified as a long, smooth pole gleaming with a blinding emerald light. On its point a very exotic-shaped blade with deadly curves similar to tongues of fire formed and black tassels flicked beneath it. She whipped the weapon around her body, spinning it so quickly between both hands the blade traced circular patterns as the green light trailed behind it. Even amidst the total chaos of beasts roaring and witches screaming and moaning, the clear tinkling of bells attached somewhere on the weapon danced lightly in the air with every sweep of the blade.

The innocent sound was obscene and totally out of place in the gory, bloody battle. Theo wasn't a religious man, but if there was ever a time an avenging angel would crash to Earth and deliver punishment, this is what it would look like.

"Capture the Mother of Shadows!"

Who?

A witch screeched from their right, doing an impressive job of not getting cleaved in half by a demon from the ground. One hand was lifted and glowing blood red as it held the blade of the massive axe and swung it at her. It snarled and slavered and leaned its full weight on the shaft of its weapon, and still the witch was able to hold it off. She was obviously one of the more powerful ones of the group and acting leader.

Her command caught Dorianne's attention, her head snapping to find the source from where she still hovered above the crater. Theo blinked, and she was gone.

The grass beneath where her feet touched ground wilted on contact, leaving a clear path of brittle, brown flora as she dashed across the clearing at an impossible speed. Her body was tilted so far forward Dorianne moved like a shadow in her own right, weaving between the lumbering legs and swinging weapons in a smoky, insubstantial way. Immediately, the rest of the witches switched their targets to try stopping Dorianne in her warpath at the expense of being downed themselves. Theo's ears rang from the rising discord filtering between the trees. He finally managed to make it to his knees again, but could only sit on his haunches in disbelief at the chaos that had broken around him in the last ten minutes.

What had I done?

Dorianne's leg snapped out as she stabbed the butt of her spear into the ground, using the momentum to whip around and knock down a cluster of witches unfortunate enough to be in her way, desperately trying to defend themselves against her demons. The way she moved so fluidly among and with her monsters was awe-inspiring, dodging and slashing out and knocking down their enemies as the demons finished them off in a brutal fashion. It was like the shadow demons were a part of her, an extension of her own body that moved on their own but also in perfect sync with her fatal dance.

So fascinated was Theo in watching the carnage erupt that, in a stupidly rookie move he would have yelled at a partner for, he didn't even notice the man creeping up just outside his periphery from behind the cabin. Nor did he have the time or coordination in his weakened state to pull his null-pistol fast enough to break loose when a burly arm wrapped around his chest and hoisted him up onto useless legs. His hands tried to grip onto the forearm but could barely get a grip on the man's grimy, sweaty skin.

"Hey, shadow bitch!" his captor screamed in his left ear. The man's breath smelled foul, like he was rotting from the inside. "Put the spear down and kneel or your fucktoy drowns in his own blood!"

Somehow his voice reached Dorianne's ears, and she swept her blade low to cut another man down at the knees for a demon to finish, falling on him with a ring-like maw of protruding teeth and two sets of clawed arms to rip him to a bloody pile of flesh. Two other demons—giant lizard-like creatures walking on two legs with massive spines from their head to the tip of their tails they swung to stab with—covered her back as Dorianne turned slowly to face Theo's captor.

Her eyes... the bitter cold of them harpooned Theo straight to his core and froze him from the inside out. She was covered, every inch of her, in shadows that fit like a second skin, but her eyes held a hollow darkness that somehow stood out from the blank expression that sat on her ageless face. The spear she held away from her body dripped viscera from tip to tip but never slipped from the hand that gripped it. Everything about her posture, that soulless stare, the tension practically vibrating from her frame, warned she was a war machine without a driver.

And now she walked through the battlefield like the Black Staff witches were beneath her attention, only swinging her weapon when someone was barreling right at her and felling them effortlessly. Those eyes never left him though. And he was too scared to look away.

Theo didn't want to be saved by this... whatever she was. He was sure Dorianne would just run that blade through the both of them and be done with it. The witch's body shook as it was pressed to his back, the knife he held digging into the side of Theo's neck hard enough to shed blood.

The decision was made, but not by Theo, his captor or Dorianne herself.

A giant, roaring ball of black fire whooshed by Dorianne so close her arm sparked mildly in retaliation from the armor she summoned to cover it. She was not its target; Theo was. Dorianne swung the blade around as if to cut the flames in half but was just a second too late. Even the man holding him was just collateral now, there wasn't enough time for him to dodge the spell cast from somewhere beyond the clearing border.

Theo's skin blistered and burned within arm's reach of the fireball. The air gasped in pain scorched his lungs, and in the next heartbeat, both he and the witch caught fire as the spell hit its mark. Theo's throat ripped loose the loudest, most tortured scream to have reached Dorianne's ears through the haze of bloodlust. For the smallest moment, the mindless fury cleared from her eyes and a forest-green gaze caught Theo's own through the unnatural flames before the spell took its toll on his very human, very mortal body.

Just as she reached out with her free hand, Theo and the bastard that had held him disintegrated into ash that scattered to a light breeze flowing through the clearing. The same wind Dorianne couldn't feel through the shadowy layer of skin-tight armor had just dispersed the only human she ever felt something for. The irony was a bitter aftertaste to the monstrous rage that boiled up her throat from deep in her chest immediately thirsting for revenge.

The last shred of her humanity burned away with Theo.

The fighting around her settled slightly, everyone in shock with the drastic turn of events. Every living being held their collective breath as if waiting to see what the fallout would be from Theo's death. Nothing could have prepared them for Dorianne.

No, no longer Dorianne.

The Mother of Shadows ate her alive.

And her first priority was killing whoever threw that dark fire.

The coven seemed to come to that conclusion shortly after her, because as she turned slowly to set her eyes on the crowd, the witches rallied toward the spellcaster, practically climbing over each other's dead bodies to huddle behind the one who showed they had enough audacity and power to cast such decimating spells. Like rats scurrying up a sinking ship to avoid their own demise.

It made for an easier target.

The Mother started with slow, purposeful steps through the clearing. Every cell in her body vibrated with unspent power. The grip on her spear tightened so hard it would have snapped an ordinary shaft. The bells on the end tinkled innocently, tapping against the gore-covered blade with every step.

Then, the steps quickened.

Faster.

Faster.

Swinging harder.

Jumping higher.

Killing more.

More.

More.

She no longer knew friend from foe. Anything her eyes laid on met the end of her blade. Demon heads flew just as often as Black Staff coven members. Bodies littered the ground to the point the witches couldn't put a foot down without getting caught on a stiffening corpse and tripping, dying before they even fell to the ground themselves. Some fled into the forest, hoping they could hide and escape from a fate they already chose.

That rage came with a cost.

Every demon she cut down returned to her as thin wisps of shadow. The weight of their magic, the burden of their power, bore down on her once again as they formed rivulets of darkness slithering behind like ducklings following their mother and adding more bulk to Dorianne's armor. Spikes grew along her shoulders in varying jagged lengths and a helmet materialized over the wild snarls of blood-slicked hair plastered to her head, two sets of spiraling horns growing from either side of her temples to stretch high above her head in a macabre copy of the demons she birthed. More tendrils wrapped themselves around her forearms, hardening to create vambraces with a distinct vine-like pattern crisscrossing from wrist to elbow.

This was the deal Dorianne had made with Death. She gave up temporary freedom to the mindless warpath she now stormed down. The entire forest filled with the screams of useless spells cast against her and the very real fear of death. Practitioners who thought they could take her down with sheer numbers now scattered like weak prey through the trees in useless attempts to escape death.

The hunt was particularly satisfying. So were their screams and pitiful cries for mercy as she cut every one of those pathetic witches down.

"You have lost yourself, Crone Grey."

The darkness seemed to coalesce, growing darker as it swirled together until two human-shaped forms stepped from it. Reflexively, Dorianne swiped her spear through the shades and made them waver like disturbed reflections in water. Not receiving the desired spray of glorious blood across her face, she snarled in a beastly way and jumped back to crouch slightly into a fighting stance.

The smaller of two bodies solidified first, heralded by the soft tinkling of bells as they stepped fully from a shimmering portal. The black robes they wore hid their faces, but an unease took root in Dorianne's stomach that hadn't been present when she was fighting the coven. It was almost like the emotion didn't even belong to her. Tendrils of her own shadow that had returned to her snapped at the air, whipping toward the intruders to fend them off. Thousands of red threads trailed behind them and glowed so brightly it hurt her eyes, even in the waning light and protective layer of armor that covered her from the retreating rays of the setting sun.

Ping. Ping ping. Ping. The sound was delicate enough to shatter, but rang through the forest as clear as the blast of a horn. With every step the smaller figure took, the bells' sounds layered on themselves until the sound drowned out the violent snarls and disjointed thoughts in Dorianne's head.

Small globes of light beckoned by the tinkling bells rose from the carnage like fireflies taking flight, floating listlessly in the air as if waiting to be caught. The figure lifted their hands with palms facing up, sleeves falling back to reveal bone-white skin etched in jagged runes and fingers stained completely black, and as they did, the lights drifted toward them. Unsure of whether to attack or run in her instinct-driven state, Dorianne's head whipped back and forth and growls rumbled from her lips as she tried to sidestep the linear paths of the glowing balls.

The threads flashed a blinding gold and triggered another wavering portal behind them, and beyond it stood toppled red pillars sitting on a smooth body of water. There was something about the sight that was so peaceful, and at the same time so heart-wrenching, watching the floating lights drift through to that impossibly beautiful place. One ball crept up from behind and touched lightly on Dorianne's shoulder—the distinct impression of a hand resting there and squeezing lightly startling her—and with it a sense of overwhelming sadness and longing washed through her and brought Dorianne to her knees with a heavy thud. Her armor, now over-burdening her with its tremendous weight , clattered and shuddered noisily from the impact.

"So many souls," the person—a woman from the sound of her voice—reached out to catch the light that had skimmed across Dorianne's shoulder in her right palm. "This one meant a lot to you, didn't it?"

Theo...

"Give...Him...Back!" Every word was garbled and mixed with bestial snarling, a fight against some kind of violent monster inside her for enough humanity to speak. Her head felt like a muddy bog she was wading through up to the hip, struggling to find herself again. The butt of the spear jabbed into the soft ground and she made to pull herself up and stagger toward the cloaked woman.

The other one stepped out in front, placing themselves between Dorianne and who was apparently his ward.

"Let her pass, Veralt."

There was a moment of hesitation. His head turned over his shoulder as if seeking a silent confirmation, or to show his obvious disagreement. Dorianne continued her stumbling regardless of his decision to move or not. She would hack him down like all the others. Her focus was singular—she had to follow that light, that feeling of acceptance it had given her, if only to experience it again for a brief moment.

Finally the man—Veralt—stepped aside only far enough to let her brush by.

"Dorianne," the woman murmured, her left hand still outstretched as if to grasp Dorianne's if she fell. "You have let the demons take too much control from you, deathwalker. You are the only one who can take it back."

No, you can't.

Shrieks of a thousand hissing voices blasted in Dorianne's mind, so loud it was painful and disconcerting. It felt impossible to concentrate on any one thought and she felt herself slipping back into the mindless rage she worked so hard to fight off.

"You can."

So the woman was able to hear the voices too.

Fuck her, they snarled. *She saddled you with a fucking curse, hauling demons around for the rest of eternity! Just let us take over, and you will never have to worry about anything again! You would never feel pain! You could be an immortal just like* her.

Their rage was her rage, their immorality becoming her own. Centuries of being oppressed and bound to one master or another left such a bitterness on their tongues, Dorianne could taste it on her own. But there was something important she had to remember. Something pulled from a dark corner of her mind, a small hand gripping tightly onto hers with both hands.

"Maybe I just want to know who I'm working with."
"Come on, I just want to talk. I just want to see you..."
"You're the most incredible miracle I've ever known."

The voice was so warm and familiar. It soothed the roiling, frantic thoughts buzzing around Dorianne's mind and settled her nerves. Her breathing slowed and muscles relaxed as she slumped to the ground at the dark figure's feet. The spear fell to the side, forgotten.

Dorianne's eyes, burning as they gradually absorbed the violent red color and returned to their usual golden-green, looked skyward. Her head felt so heavy, hanging back on a loose neck and covered with the demonic-looking helmet that gripped it. Tears trickled down her temples, but she didn't really know why.

All she knew was that she lost something very important to her. But she had to carry on without it. She had to *live*.

The shadows thrashed and riled wildly around her, rising like inky smoke from the fallen bodies of demons scattered throughout the forest and glade that had yet to be absorbed. As one, they swarmed together and fell upon Dorianne as a terrifying leviathan would swallow a ship. No matter how much she braced herself, avoiding the onslaught of a thousand memories of a thousand horrible lifetimes was impossible. The darkness soaked into her bones and flowed through her blood.

Slowly, painfully, they settled back into her skin, digging into her bones and flowing through her veins as the collective entity of the demon horde filled the dark cavern Dorianne had sanctioned them to in her mind.

Fucking ridiculous, Shady nagged in their usual grating chorus of demonic voices. *We allow you power beyond your wildest dreams and eternal life, and you spit in our faces! Being tied to a worthless human is the worst insult we have ever received, and one day that bitch Azrael will know to fear our infinite—*

"Enough."

One word. All it took was one word from Death to silence the shadows. They cowered in reluctant respect at the domineering aura of the small woman standing before Dorianne. And it galled them.

Dorianne slumped forward and barely caught herself on the palms of her hands before falling face-first onto the ground. The cost of absorbing all those shades took an enormous toll on her physical body as well as her psyche. Her energy was flagging.

Just at the edge of her vision, a dark cloak stopped in front of her. "We must go, Crone. My presence will be noted by Hell if I intervene much more." Something light and cool brushed the top of her bent head. Maybe a hand? "I hope you find peace in knowing that not all is lost. The one you care for will return at the right time."

The one I care for? Surely, she couldn't mean...

Dorianne's head lifted up to Death. Her eyes widened, finally realizing who she could be talking about. "Th... Theo is... How could I?"

Nothing was making sense. Theo was... dead?

Azrael backed away, her companion joining at her side again as they turned to the looming portal behind them. Those flying lights—souls, she now understood—were almost done trickling through the shimmering portal as well. Just before the cloaked pair stepped through, Azrael turned her head to speak over a shoulder.

"Thank you, Crone Grey."

The Penance

Restoration Era, Year 223

F ive years had passed in the blink of an eye, but they didn't bleed together as much as they used to in Dorianne's memory. Occasionally, she would even don a full-length coat or long cardigan and venture out to the nearby town when the sun had fully hidden behind the horizon, of course. Shady was content to hide beneath the outer layer of her clothes instead of looming over her shoulder as they usually did. And they liked to comment on people passing by as she walked down the main thoroughfare.

Why does she have so many children? Doesn't that woman know those little heathens lead to insanity?

That man has impeccable taste in fashion.
He needs a haircut, badly.
Mmmmm, this woman looks delectable.

She didn't mind the chatter. On average, Shady had become a much more pleasant companion to talk to than... Well, better than before. Dorianne didn't like to dwell on the day that had undoubtedly been a turning point in their symbiotic relationship. While she had gained a more amicable Shady, she had also lost someone more dear than she could ever truly place value on. She was shocked when Killian Tate himself came to her door the very next day by portal in full formal regalia, his black uniform with the gold trim and SIA insignia stitched over his heart almost as heartbreaking a sight as when Theo took his last breath. He had taken Theo's body home—or at least, the ashes left that Dorianne was able to collect—along with an escort of six agents, also dressed in somber black.

All of her tears had been shed by then. Dorianne could only watch from the doorway as they gently lifted his body from the bed in her guest room and lowered him into that horrible box. She burned the bed immediately after they left, frame and all. The room still held scorch marks on the floor and up the wall and smoke damage everywhere else, ash wedged between the floorboards that she didn't bother to dig out beyond a courtesy sweep.

As adventurous as she was now, Dorianne never expected to need a bed in that room again. While she didn't think Azrael would outright lie to her about Theo's rebirth, her hopes were not particularly high that he would find her again, in a world full of people and opportunities she had no interest in exploring.

Dorianne bided her time, and studied more powerful ways to utilize Shady's magic to compliment her own. She had sat dormant for far too many years, content to be a lap dog to the SIA in lieu of tracking down that traitorous sister of hers. But now, she waited. Black Staff would consume itself with they ever-starving greed, and once the coven is nothing more than a bony corpse Dylan will come looking for her to harvest more magic with her savage rituals.

The trap had been set. Dylan couldn't stay away forever, knowing that I had even stronger magic to harvest now. She will come, thinking I had grown complacent and docile and depressed. When she does, I will fucking crush her.

So five years became ten in a soothing, predictable pattern of days spent foraging for spellcasting and discovering the endless wonders of magic. Through the years Dorianne had to expand her cottage's shelves countless times to make room for all the precious hand-bound tomes that held her research.

Dorianne had become something of a local legend--the Woman of the Wood--that the townspeople gossiped about or told passing travelers tales of. Once a little girl had been riding her bike along a trail close to the treeline and hit a sharp rock, breaking some of the spokes and sending her tumbling to the ground. She had been fine enough to run off crying and left the bike discarded on the side of the path, so Dorianne waited until nightfall to collect the bike, repair it, and set it just outside the forest. Someone had taken the bike into town a few days later—according to a report from Shady—and the girl was riding it along the same trail the very next day. Snapped sandals, broken jewelry, unraveling baskets, Dorianne wandered the forest looking for things to mend and set them on or around a particular flat rock for their owner to eventually find. People then left things on the rock for Dorianne—treasures that obviously meant a lot to them, folded in scraps of cloth or left in baskets—in hopes it would return to them in perfect condition.

She didn't mind. It brought joy, sitting in the darkened shadows and watching someone walk up to the rock and find their items fixed, sometimes bringing tears to their eyes. Woman of the Wood was a much more pleasant moniker than Mother of Shadows. But it also meant the more curious would come venturing into the forest to find her themselves, which she was not interested in.

She had been sitting on a stool with her easel in the clearing in front of the log cabin, restoring an old painting of someone's grandfather who had recently passed—according to the note left with it on her rock—when the most unsuspected and yet most welcome soul stumbled into it.

He was quite tall and somewhat lanky, sporting some khaki brown shorts and a light green crew neck shirt with a satchel thrown across his shoulder. Seeing him standing there, almost in the exact same spot Theo had come through when he forced his way through her barrier all those years ago, stunned her into paralyzed silence. They stared at each other over the dancing wildflowers and newly sprouted grass of late spring, the weak light of the setting sun dappling them with tiny drops of gold that shifted with the moving leaves above them.

He was the first to break the growing—and uncomfortable—silence. "Uh... hi? Are you the wood lady?"

Dorianne blinked. The stranger blinked. Then, completely shocking them both, a great peel of laughter burst from her lips and she rocked back on the stool, nearly falling off the back with the force of it. Eyes closed, tears streaming from them, brush carefully held away from the painting so as not to ruin it, her laughs filled the whole clearing and completely mesmerized the young man.

He had never seen anything more beautiful, and so authentic, as Dorianne howling with her mirth.

"The... wood... lady?" She finally gasped brokenly, holding her stomach and she tried to recover her breath.

His own humor finally caught up, and the man chuckled a little at himself. "I should have worked that out some more in my head, huh? Sorry, I didn't mean to be rude, Miss... Er, Woman of the Wood."

The sheer level of awkwardness made him all the more endearing. The man's face glowed bright red underneath the heavy dusting of freckles across his nose and cheeks, his eyes the exact shade of hazel Theo's was. Dorianne didn't remember enjoying a conversation, however stilted this one was, since... maybe the first time she spoke through her door to Theo. That felt like a lifetime ago. But there was something about the aura of her unexpected guest that reminded her a lot of him.

"Dorianne."

"Pardon?" He seemed baffled.

"My name," she smiled at him, "is Dorianne."

"Wow... I mean, of course you have a name."

"What is yours?"

It seemed an innocent enough question, wholly appropriate after giving her own. But the terrified look on his face was priceless, and another bark of laughter left her lips.

"I'm not going to turn you into a cow and eat you," Dorianne teased. "Well... not yet, anyways. I'm not hungry right now, but that could change if this conversation lasts too long."

"Theodore!" The name burst from him in a rush. He was visibly frazzled, perhaps thinking she would turn him into some edible creature. "It's... it's Theodore Ashe."

"Charmed."

"Really? Am I gonna die?"

Her eyes rolled at the exaggerated fear in his hazel eyes. Wavy pieces of dark brown hair had fallen across his forehead when he stumbled into her clearing that he hadn't even bothered with brushing away. The disheveled appearance was, dare she think it, very cute. But at the risk of the paints on her canvas drying past the point of being able to blend, Dorianne picked up the brush from where she had dropped it in the grass and rinsed it thoroughly in a wooden bowl. She wanted to finish the restoration before morning and let it dry for the day so it could be returned to the flat rock tomorrow night.

"You can carry on trembling in fear over there, or busy yourself with something else in my forest. I have work to do as the wood lady, you know."

The taunt hit its mark. Theodore's shoulders relaxed minutely and an exasperated look overtook his face before he could think twice about it. "I'm not going to live that down, am I?"

"Probably not. I have an excellent memory."

"Of course you would."

"So tell me, Theodore Ashe," Dorianne spoke while she carried on with repainting the curve of a cheek. "What were you planning to do once you found me? Was there something you needed repaired?"

The brush in her hand almost moved on its own, with how long she had spent losing herself in the craft. It was painful at first, just after Theo's death, to even pick up a brush without thinking about the last portrait she had painted. The one of his thoughtful expression that transformed to his last moments of life, with Dorianne staring down at him with a gaze full of hatred and bloodthirst. She had fought so hard to avoid that future. In the end, she may have made it all the more inevitable with her cowardice.

Her question appeared to have jogged Theodore's memory. With a little "oh," he pulled the satchel around and dug into it until he found whatever it was he brought with him. "I found this notebook in a neighbor's storage room, in one of the boxes underneath a bunch of blankets. It looks like maybe the damp or something got to it, but I was hoping you could, I don't know, restore it somehow. The pages are practically falling out."

It was a small book, no wider than his palm and maybe half as long as his large, tanned hand. The cover looked to be some kind of leather with how rugged it looked, and the edges of the pages peeking out were tattered and stained. And the faint magic emanating from it... Dorianne knew who this had belonged to long before the man walked up to place it in her outstretched hand. That same aura emanated from Theodore and soothed the ache in her heart.

Dorianne opened the cover gingerly, holding it as carefully as a newborn bird cupped in her pale hands as she looked for the initials etched into the leather.

T.S.

And before the very first page was another folded piece that had been tucked into it, the paper a completely different texture but just as known to her. She handed it to the man to unfold himself; the curiosity leaking from him was almost palpable. Theodore's warm eyes widened in disbelief, bouncing from her gentle smile as she watched him to the page and back again.

"I don't... this is... how?" Poor man. She was sure what he saw was hard to grasp. Like jumping into a story halfway told, the context was missing entirely.

But Dorianne's smile turned a little mischievous, the wrinkle in her nose the same as the drawing he held. "It's a long story. But one I'm happy to tell. Would you like to stay for tea?"

To Be Continued...

www.ingramcontent.com/pod-product-compliance
Lightning Source LLC
LaVergne TN
LVHW012018060526
838201LV00061B/4356